The Outcast
Book I

by

Selma Lagerlöf

The Outcast
Book I
by Selma Lagerlöf

ISBN: 978-93-64288-83-5

Published by

DOUBLE 9 BOOKS

2/13-B, Ansari Road
Daryaganj, New Delhi – 110002
info@double9books.com
www.double9books.com
Tel. 011-40042856

ABOUT THE AUTHOR

Selma Lagerlöf (1858–1940) was a renowned Swedish author and the first woman to win the Nobel Prize in Literature. Her works are celebrated for their imaginative storytelling, integration of Swedish folklore, and exploration of human themes.: Lagerlöf gained fame with her debut novel, Gösta Berling's Saga (1891), a rich and imaginative story set in 19th-century Sweden that combines historical fiction with fairy-tale elements. Some of her other significant works include The Wonderful Adventures of Nils (1906–1907), a children's book about a young boy's journey through Sweden, and The Outcast (1925), which delves into themes of social exclusion and redemption. Selma Lagerlöf's contributions to literature have had a lasting impact, both in Sweden and internationally. Her unique voice and imaginative storytelling have influenced numerous writers and continue to captivate readers. In addition to the Nobel Prize, Lagerlöf's work has been recognized for its cultural significance and literary quality. Her stories have been adapted into various forms, including film and theater.

Selma Lagerlöf remains a celebrated figure in literature, known for her profound and imaginative narratives that offer deep insights into the human experience and the cultural heritage of Sweden.

CONTENTS

GRIMÖN 7

IN GOD'S HOUSE 17

FATHER, MOTHER, AND SON 22

THE "NAIAD" 31

THE SCHOOLHOUSE 35

THE STONEHILLS 39

THE SEA 44

SAILING 50

LESS THAN THE LEAST 62

GRIMÖN

ON THE island of Grimön, among the rocks and reefs of the western coast of Sweden, there lived, some years back, a man and his wife. The two were much unlike each other.

Joel Elversson, the husband, was the elder of the pair by fifteen years or so. Ill-favoured to look at, heavy and slow, he had always been, and age had not improved him. His wife, on the other hand, was still as neat and pleasant a little body as ever; far from having lost her looks, she seemed almost as pretty now, at fifty, as she had been at twenty.

One fine Sunday evening the couple were sitting on a big flat rock just outside their house, chatting together at their ease. Joel was a man who enjoyed hearing his own voice, and delivered his words with care. Just now he was giving his wife at some length the contents of an article he had read in the paper. The little woman listened, but her thoughts were not following very closely.

"Eh," she thought to herself, "he's a wonderful head has Joel, to be sure. How he can get all that out of a bit of print in a newspaper.... Pity he can't put his learning to some use for us both, instead of others."

Involuntarily she glanced across at the house. It was a good-sized place in itself, but in such a state of dilapidation as to be largely uninhabitable; the pair lived now in one small outbuilding, which the previous tenants, sea-captains all, had used for kitchen and larder.

"If only he'd had a liking for the sea," went on Mor Elversson to herself, "like his father and grandfather before him. He'd have laid by something now, and we'd be able to look forward to old age in ease and comfort. But he's always been set on farming and field work and such, and little enough it's brought us."

She did not move from her place while her husband was speaking, but her little head, that moved quickly and easily as a bird's, turned slightly as she glanced over the patches of cornfield and potato, little islands of growth among the barren rock that formed the greater part of the island.

Every little strip of cultivation was her husband's work; the very soil was, in a manner of speaking, his creation. He had brought endless boatloads of earth and manure to Grimön, in the firm conviction that he must one day reap a rich reward for his pains.

"All that trouble for so many bits of earth, and poor at that," thought his wife to herself. "Needs but one good northerly gale at Whitsuntide, and all the sowing and planting'd be nowhere Nay, 'tis to the sea we should look for our daily bread, living here as we do. There's neither right nor reason in it else."

Another movement of the quick little head, and she was looking out through the space between the tumbledown old house and the cottage, over the broad, gleaming surface of the water beyond.

"Ay, the sea," she sighed. "'Tis different with that. Freights and cargoes and good money paid. If I'd been a man, I'd have gone to sea from the first, and never taken up with the farm work at all. And here we're getting old and older, and what's to become of us when we're past work? There's none of the children'd stay at home to toil and moil that away—and small blame to them for that."

The last words must have been spoken aloud, for her husband turned sharply toward her. He had been describing the perils and hardships of an English expedition recently returned from the Arctic, and broke off now in the middle of a sentence.

"You're not listening," he said. But it was doubtless not the first time he had found himself talking to deaf ears, for he seemed neither surprised nor annoyed.

"Indeed I was," his wife assured him. "I was thinking this very moment how fine you talk, and how you'd do for a preacher."

"I don't know about that," said the husband, with a laugh. "If I can't keep one listener from thinking of all and sundry when I'm preaching, how'd I manage with a congregation?"

"But I was listening," his wife protested, somewhat discomfited. "I've got it all in my head now. How they lost their ship the very first winter and managed to build a snow house, and had to stay and live there for over a year, till all their food was gone, and they were chewing bits of hide."

There was a note of vexation in her voice, and her mouth twitched in a way it often did when anything troubled her.

"Wonder how it would feel," suggested her husband, casually, "if 'twas one of our own blood had been there starving in a snow hut."

The woman glanced at him sharply. What did he mean by that now? Something, surely. But Joel sat staring before him, with no trace of expression in his rheumy eyes.

"Well, if we were to spend all our time sitting thinking of other folks' troubles, there'd be little pleasure in life," she said, apologetically. "And, anyhow, they were saved in the end."

"That's true," Joel admitted. "There was a ship went out to find them, and they're safe back in England now."

"And all the honour and glory, and live happy ever after," concluded his wife.

To her mind, there was nothing to be so serious about when all had come well at last. But her husband went on without changing his tone.

"I dreamt last night about our boy Sven," he said. "Dreamt he came and stood by my bed and said I'd done him a sore wrong. I won't say if I've any gift of dreaming true as a rule, and I don't know if there's anything in this or not. But it's a queer thing, all the same, to see his name in the paper here to-day."

The last words were spoken carelessly, as if the speaker were thinking only of himself. But from that moment he had no reason to complain of want of attention in his listener. His wife came close to him and deluged him with questions: Where was the name? What was it he had dreamt? Was there really anything about their boy Sven? Her voice grew shrill, her nose flushed, and tears stood in her eyes.

Had it been any other of their children, she would have been less easily moved. But it was different with Sven. They had given the boy away, when nine years old, to an English gentleman and his lady, who had come sailing along the coast in a yacht. The strangers had simply fallen in love with the child, and had promised, if he were entrusted to them, to bring him up as their own, as a rich gentleman, and make him their heir.

It was a wonderful prospect for the lad; his parents had felt that for his own sake they dared not refuse. If he stayed with them, he would have none to help him but themselves. And he was a bright child, with a clever head; they had often agreed that he would surely get on in the world if he had but the chance in his upbringing.

Seventeen years now since they had let him go, and during all that time they had heard nothing from him. Never a letter, never a word of greeting. They knew no more of him than if he had lain at the bottom of the sea.

"See there," said the man, handing across the paper to his wife. "List of those saved. Here it is. 'Sven E. Springfield.'"

"Yes, yes. 'Sven E. Springfield'—it's there, right enough."

"And that can't mean anything but Sven Elversson Springfield," Joel went on. "His own name, mine, and his foster-father's. There's no mistake about that."

Mor Elversson crushed the paper close. At that moment she felt that the son she had given up to others of her own free will was dearest of all her children.

"Why didn't you say straight out at once that Sven was there?" she said, reproachfully. "I wasn't listening. Now you'll have to tell it all over again."

Joel seemed somewhat at a loss. He had thought to tell her the whole story before saying a word about Sven; it would have been easier so. Then he could have seen how she took it, and acted accordingly.

However, he must tell her now. And he went on to explain all she wished to know. What was meant by the eightieth degree of latitude, for instance. And she listened, growing eager on her son's behalf for the honours to be won, and thinking surely he and his comrades must have reached farther than any before them. And what had they lived on after the ship had gone down with all their stores? The story of how the relief expedition had found them that summer, on the shores of Melville Island, had to be repeated over and over again.

"Oh, what he must have had to go through in all that time!" she exclaimed. "No, 'tis a wicked thing to give away one's own child to strangers."

"But he's made his fortune now, I suppose," she went on, relieved. "And they'll give him a host of medals and orders and all."

Soon she began to wonder how the boy had been received in England on his return.

"Millions of people came out to see them," said Joel. "'Arctic explorers' homecoming.'"

He felt ill at ease, anxious, and in fear. All their future depended on how he framed his words now; if he could say the thing as it must be said.

"If only we could have been there too," said his wife. "If I could but have stood at a street corner and seen him go by."

"No need for you to have stood at street corners," said Joel. "It says here there was a special steamer for parents and relatives to meet them."

The look of joy faded suddenly from her face. "Eh, Joel," she sighed. "Little good it would have been if we'd been there. They'd never have let you nor me go on that steamer boat. *She* wouldn't have let us."

"*She*" was Mor Elversson's word for the English lady that had taken away her son. She had never forgiven her for forbidding her son to write to his parents. And in her thoughts this stranger woman had become a monster.

"I doubt but they'd have let us see him, all the same," said Joel.

It was some relief to him, in a way, that his wife laid stress on little details such as this. He needed time to collect his thoughts before he could break the news to her. All their future depended on how it was said and taken; he told himself this again and again, as if to urge his mind to the effort.

"Never believe it!" cried the woman, stubbornly, with a toss of her head. "When she never so much as let him write a line all these years. And I doubt but he's little thought for us, anyway. Nine years old he was, when he went away, and sense enough, if he'd cared, to write without her knowing. But it's plain enough; she's put it into his head how we were common folk, and not the sort for a little young gentleman to be asking about."

All her joy was gone and vanished now; the thoughts that had plagued her so often in the past came back with renewed force.

"I'll admit," said her husband—"I'll admit it's a strange thing Sven shouldn't have written a single word to us all that time. And it may well be 'twas their fault that wouldn't let him. I heard something up at the church to-day."

The woman said no word. She was too sick at heart to speak.

"This is going badly," said Joel to himself. "If she's in that humour, there's little hope anyway."

"The Pastor's had news from England," he said aloud. And now again he was touching on a matter he had thought to leave until his wife was more prepared, and in the mood to take it better. But there seemed no help for it now. "Pastor asked me to go along home with him. 'Twas he that gave me the newspaper here."

"The Pastor?"

"Yes. Wanted to talk to me about Sven."

"Huh! What do I care! 'Tis all the same now, the way he's turned out."

Joel made no reply to this, and they sat for a long time in silence. At last the woman burst out violently:

"I never knew the like of you for making a poor body curious. What was it Pastor's heard from England?"

"It was news of Sven. And Pastor's coming himself to tell you about it this evening."

The woman sprang to her feet. "Pastor himself—coming here! Well, of all the wonders.... And you sitting there and never said a word of it till now!"

She took a pace toward the house, thinking to look round and see that all was clean and in order. Then suddenly she stopped.

"What's he coming here for?" she said. "There must be something wrong."

She cast a keen glance at her husband, as if trying to look into his mind and read the thoughts within.

"Maybe Sven's turned softer now," she said, "after being up there in the ice and chewing bits of hide. Maybe he's wishful to come and see us, after all. But, mark my words, this time *I* say no! If we weren't good enough for him before, we're no better now."

"Be careful of your words," said her husband, warningly. "You never know but you might be sorry after." He felt a growing anger toward her for speaking so violently, and taking the whole thing differently from what he would have done himself.

Mor Elversson had forgotten all about seeing to the house now. Her husband's last words could mean but one thing—she had guessed rightly.

"And do you know what's the news Pastor's coming to tell?"

"I know something—yes."

"Was it himself told you to read out all that in the paper for me to hear?"

"Well, no. He was going to tell you himself, I take it. But I reckoned it was best you should know a little before he came, and be prepared."

"And just as well," said his wife. "Well that I knew of it in time. I might have been forgetting myself and saying good-day and welcome before I knew, and been sorry for it after."

Joel felt his anger increasing. "She'll spoil it all beyond mending," he thought to himself, "and it's all our future to think of. Eh, she'll never be wiser, only growing worse and worse for every year."

"I fancy Pastor 'll be glad to hear you can talk so careless like about Sven. All one to you ... well, 'twill make it easier for him to say what he's got to say."

"Easier? ..." repeated the woman, and her voice seemed harsher even than before. "What d'you mean by that?"

"Why, it looks as if Sven's in trouble after all. That procession, when they came home, that was to be last Sunday, and so it was, as fine as could be. Next day, too, there was banquets and invitations and things—and then all of a sudden it stopped. They'd come back from the Arctic all right, but folk were beginning to say strange things about them. Ugly things."

The woman's face set hard.

"You mean to tell me he's done something wrong?" she murmured between clenched teeth.

"Took down all the flowers and flags and stuff, and put a stop to everything. One day they could hardly make a way through the streets for folk crowding round to cheer the sight of them; and the next, those same folks ready to spit on them."

Mor Elversson raised her head.

"Well, I never heard ..." she cried. "I doubt it would have been better for him to have stayed with his own flesh and blood after all."

"Remember," said her husband, speaking more forcefully now, "it's not the first time such things have happened away on expeditions like that. They were starving, and mad with hunger, and didn't rightly know what they were doing. And then one of them couldn't stand it any longer, and took and cut his throat, and after that, well ..."

"Well? They ate him up, I suppose you mean?"

She spoke the words coldly, without a trace of excitement. Her heart was full of bitterness and disgust.

"They were no more accountable, really, than folk in a madhouse," said her husband. "And it says here in the paper they couldn't bring themselves to go on. Only started like."

"And Sven was in it, too?"

"When anything like that happens, they take good care all's in it. They made him do like the rest. But that was all."

"And now," cried his wife, with an indescribable contempt in her voice—"now I know what it is Pastor's got to say. Sven's not good enough for *her* now, and so he's got Pastor to come and persuade us to let him come back here. Isn't that it?"

"I daresay that would be best, if it could be done," said Joel, slowly.

"But I say no!" cried his wife. "I say no! He shan't come back here because he's nowhere else to go. He forgot all about us as long as he was well off and comfortable; don't let him think we're anxious to have him now. Poor and old we may be, and needing help. But we'll not have a son that's done things so nobody else will own him."

Joel Elversson looked at his wife, with anger and impatience in his eyes. He was old and weak, and it would have been a grand thing for him to have a son at home able to work. His wife's feeling seemed to him childish and unreasonable; she was obstinate; she was downright wicked. "Wait," he thought to himself. "Wait, and you'll soon hear something more to your mind."

"Just as I said," he went on aloud. "Pastor won't find it so hard, after all, to tell you what was in the letter."

"It—isn't it what I thought, then?" asked his wife in a milder tone. Her stubbornness was shaken by his evident anger and disapproval.

He looked at her sternly.

"Would you like me to tell you myself, or wait till Pastor comes?"

And in his impatience to punish her for her want of affection, he did not wait for an answer, but went on:

"They live in London—the Springfields. And Sven had gone back home to them there. But when the ugly stories began to get about, the father sent a paper with the news up to him—and a loaded revolver with it."

"And the mother—what about her? Did she know he'd sent it?"

"She knew—yes."

"And—and what then?"

"Then—why, it came about as they wished. That's all."

"And now—he's dead."

"Now—now you know what Pastor had to tell you," said her husband.

"And she," cried the poor mother—"she that was not his mother at all, but had had him with her all those years, she let him kill himself, when he'd done no wrong?"

She turned on her husband fiercely.

"You lie!" she cried. "It is not true!"

"I'd have said those very words myself an hour ago. I wouldn't have believed that a woman could be so heartless. But since I've heard you, now, I can believe it."

"But—but he hadn't only them to look to. He'd his mother and father here."

"Most likely he thought we'd take it the same way. And he wasn't so far wrong, it seems."

Mor Elversson turned away, and sat down on the rock. The tears ran down her cheeks. "Sven's dead," she said, "dead. No mother but a woman with a heart of stone—and she let him die."

She sat awhile, weeping and moaning.

"O God, why did we ever let him go? And that woman to send him to his death for nothing! When it was the others that made him ..."

"You'd better try and be calm a bit," said her husband. "Here's the Pastor coming. The boat's just putting in."

"Tell him I know all about it. He can go back again."

"Can't very well do that, when he's been at the trouble to come."

Joel walked away, and came back a moment later with the Pastor and a young man.

The priest walked up to the weeping woman.

"Joel tells me you've heard already, Mor Elversson," he said. "About Sven. He was concerned in a very unpleasant business, and his adopted parents sent him away."

Mor Elversson had risen to curtsey to the Pastor. She still held a corner of her apron to her eyes, but, for all her weeping, she caught a glimpse of the stranger with him.

"It's Sven," said a voice within her. "Sven...."

A host of thoughts crowded into her mind. She realized that Joel had lied to her, in his anger at her heartlessness. She felt, too, that she would never be able to overcome the sorrow she had felt on hearing that her son had tasted human flesh. She saw that they would have to keep this son at home with them now, since no one else would have him in their service. But in the midst of all these cold reflections she saw how thin and pale the boy looked, how his eyes begged her sympathy, and a wave of pity and love rose in her heart.

"Eh, Joel, Joel," she thought. "Always strange in his ways. He's shown me now what I am; made me see what I really feel. I know now, that for all the boy's been away from us all these years, and come back in disgrace, I can't but love him all the same."

And, without a word to the Pastor, she stepped forward to her son and bade him welcome, her husband watching her anxiously the while.

"Surely," she said, in her gentlest voice, "it was just for this that the trouble came—that Joel and I might have you back again."

IN GOD'S HOUSE

SVEN ELVERSSON, the man who had been greeted as a son by the two old folk at Grimön, sat in the church at Applum, thanking God that he had found a place of refuge where he was not looked upon with horror and disgust.

On the lonely, rocky little island with its two poor inhabitants, he had no fear of encountering that downward curve of the lips that signified loathing. His father was an old man, and felt no disgust toward him, having no strong feelings any longer in that way. His mother was sensitive as ever, but she loved him.

The church in which he sat was an old wooden building, the ceiling decorated with a great picture of the Judgment. And every time he looked up he found himself involuntarily gazing at a big, black, grinning devil, who was thrusting fuel under a cauldron filled with sinners boiling in a sulphurous broth. Sven Elversson knew that particular fiend of old, from the time when he had been in that very church seventeen years before. A striking feature was the long tail, cloven in three at the tip, which he used with great dexterity to stir the boiling mess.

As a child he had often let his fancy play about the figure of this master cook, who managed so skilfully to tend his fire and his pot at the same time. Now, however, other thoughts were in his mind. If all those who every Sunday looked up at that merry spirit of the infernal kitchens at his boiling were suddenly told that there, in their midst, sat one of their fellows who had actually tasted human flesh, they would hardly let him remain there long.

There was one thing—he could find no other to compare with it—which civilised human beings could not do. Murder, adultery, cruelty, theft; these they could commit. They were not above such things as drunkenness, rape, treason, espionage. Such things as these were of daily occurrence. There were, no doubt, those who would shrink from any such crime, but the things were done. *One* of mankind's ancient sins there was which no longer existed in civilized countries—a thing too loathsome for any to contemplate. And that he had done. Yes, he was more to be abhorred than any fiend.

The only soul in the church, beyond his parents, who knew the reason of Sven Elversson's homecoming was the Priest. But the Pastor had received him kindly on the previous Sunday, showed him sympathy, and spoken with his father; had gone with him out to Grimön, and been pleased to see his mother's affectionate welcome—and had approved the idea of his remaining at home with his parents. The Priest had shown himself throughout as a tolerant and generous man.

To-day, as the Pastor entered his church, his eyes fell on Sven Elversson, the man from the starvation camp at Melville Island. And at sight of him he felt a stifling sensation in his throat.

He had helped this man, and done what he could for him; he had been glad to be the means of bringing him back to his home, and finding a refuge for an unfortunate who was made to suffer for what he had been forced to commit; a fellow creature in such desperate straits that he might otherwise have turned to suicide. But he had not thought to see him here in church.

At the vicarage, he would not have hesitated to receive him if he had come. But this he could not endure. The man had eaten human flesh—had been guilty of something heathenish, abominable. Surely, he ought to have understood himself that his presence there was intolerable.

A moment after, he reproached himself for his thoughts, accused himself of uncharitableness, and called to mind how Christ had bidden all sinners come to Him. He strove to rouse more sympathy in himself; he thought of the poor sinner's gentle, kindly bearing, and checked his first impulse to send the verger with a message asking him to leave the church. He went through the service, and delivered his sermon as usual, but could not free himself from a feeling of abhorrence.

The words he had to speak clung to his palate; he had to pause once or twice in his sermon and clear his tongue before he could go on. It was as if the taste of something loathsome actually filled his mouth; he seemed to be witnessing the scene as it had happened: the group of starving men flinging themselves upon the body of the suicide.

He would have felt nothing of this had it not been for the presence of the man himself there in the church. But the feeling had come upon him now, and he felt himself helpless in its grasp. He clenched his hands in strife with himself, turned in the pulpit so as to keep the figure of Sven Elversson away from sight; he strove to read the sermon as he had written it, forced himself to concentrate his thoughts upon his words, and suddenly the trouble was gone, and he felt at ease once more.

But now it chanced that he came to a passage in the sermon dealing with falsehood, and how far it might be justified in certain cases. And at once his thoughts turned to Grimön, and the manner in which Joel Elversson had brought his wife to realize her true feelings. It was his custom frequently to illustrate his sermons with episodes from real life, and in doing so, he did not write down the story beforehand, but told it in such words as came to him at the moment. And now it occurred to him that the little happening at Grimön might be used by way of example.

He had had no thought before of using it, but now, carried away by his subject, he took it up.

He had not been speaking long before a warning thought crossed his mind—it was perhaps hardly well to make the matter known to the whole congregation. True, no one had asked him to keep it a secret. Nevertheless, he felt uneasy, and sought for some way of altering the story as he went on, but could find none, and told it as it was. He tried to emphasize only that part which bore on his subject, of falsehood and justification, but here again he failed, and told the very thing that should have remained unsaid, making known the entire affair to all those present.

At first, he felt ashamed of what he had done, then suddenly he was seized with a sense of exultation at thus treading underfoot the unclean spirit that had dared to appear in the church itself. "Despicable worm!" he thought. "That such a creature should ever presume to enter into my church—into the house of God."

He had struggled against the sense of loathing; now, it had crept upon him unawares and overwhelmed him.

All next day the Priest was ill at ease. He had not acted as a man should, with proper self-control. He had behaved like a child, like a savage, giving way to instinct at once.

In vain he tried to find some way in which to repair what he had done; it could not be altered now. He must wait until some opportunity offered. The more he made of the affair just now, the worse it would be.

But what a power—what a terrible power—lay in this sense of loathing, that it could thus overwhelm a man, as it had done with him, at the very moment when he stood as teacher and spiritual guide in a Christian church, speaking to Christian souls!

The little party from Grimön left the church as the preacher descended from the pulpit.

Once outside, they stopped involuntarily, and stood a moment by the church door, looking around.

The church stood in the middle of a level, open plain—an unusual thing in that part of the country. Not of very wide extent, but still considerable. One could see from one side to the other, and mark the doings of one's neighbours, yet, for all that, it was large enough to furnish ground for church and vicarage, and a score of homesteads and farms round about.

The plain was walled in by gray, rocky hills on every side—not very high, but still considerable. Both the north wind and the west could force their way across the barrier, yet it sufficed to shut out the view of everything beyond, even to the mountain peaks.

The whole plain was cut up into field on field of cultivated ground— and these were neither large nor small, but of a size to suit the standing of honest peasant farmers. And here and there among the fields were buildings, red and blue and white, likewise of an equable, respectable size. No big mansions dominating all the rest, and, on the other hand, no poor cottages such as might serve to exalt the appearance of the others, and make for pride in those who dwelt there.

As for the vegetation, it could not be called luxuriant, for there were no trees to be seen, whether as woods on the hillsides, or in groups on the plain, or set in rows along the waysides. On the other hand, it could not be denied that it was a fertile soil, as it lay there now in its autumn glory—a waving sea of wheat and grass and peas and beans and clover.

Almost in the middle of the plain stood the church, from which the Grimön folk themselves had just, as it were, been driven out. It was an old-fashioned wooden building, that could not be called altogether ugly, for it had a slender little tower rising up boldly, and leading the mind heavenward. On the other hand, it was hardly beautiful, by reason of its dark, heavy nave, that weighed down the soul to earth.

And in the stone-walled enclosure about the church itself, a gray-striped cat wandered to and fro while the three stood without. A handsome animal, well marked, with close, fine fur, and a pleasant softness in all its movements.

But as they watched it, there seemed to be something uncanny about the way its limbs moved under the soft skin. It was not only that it moved so silently, or that its green slits of eyes, as it looked at them, were so veiled and without expression. The thing was hateful because it was so smooth and soft and pleasant-looking, while all the time it thought of nothing but stealing and killing.

And as they looked, the cat seemed to grow and stretch itself and expand, until it rose so high as to shut out sight of the wall of hills. And as the creature grew, it purred and hummed and made all manner of playful, easy movements—and the horror of it increased.

And they saw that the beast was the loathing that had arisen about them—the loathing that was to grow and grow till it spread over all the plain, that could find no better soil for its growth than here, shut in within narrow bounds, where all things were level, equable, even....

Mor Nathalia Elversson faced round toward the church, and, scraping with her nails at the red-painted wooden wall, tore loose a few splinters, which she laid between the leaves of her prayer book.

"Here in this church I was christened," she said, "when I was a week old. And here I was confirmed as a young girl. Here I was married, and here, like as not, they'll read the burial service over me. But, till that day comes, I'll enter there no more, as long as the shame of this day's left to endure."

FATHER, MOTHER, AND SON

AS THE two old people at Grimön came to know their stranger son, they wondered at him for many things.

"I tell you this, Joel," said Mor Elversson to her husband one day, "that if *I*'d been taken away and brought up amongst gentlefolks as one of themselves, and then all suddenly had to lay it all by, and come to live on such fare as we can give, after being used to all manner of dainties; if I'd had to leave all that and turn to helping you in the fields and never so much as time to read in a book, nor ever change a word with finer folks, but only a pair of ninnies like you and me—if it was me was come to that, I'd be sullen and hard from morning to night, that I would. And I doubt but you'd be the same."

Joel agreed that he would find it hard to be otherwise in such a case.

"And then look at Sven," went on his wife. "As if there was never a thought of such in his head. And he's not grieving over money and friends he's lost or that sort. Never seems to trouble him that he's no sort of pleasure nor enjoyment to turn to. He can go about here laughing and chaffing with me, and arguing with you, as if he'd never thought nor longing for better company. Every day the same—gentle and humble and glad as any God's lamb. There's but one thing I can see that plagues him."

"Well, as for that, I can't think any the worse of him for feeling so. It's the disgrace that's ever on his mind—and that's a sore thing for any man to bear."

"Ay, that's true. And a cruel thing it is that folk can't get used to him like, so he can't go over to the post, or into a store, but there's some that curl lips at him or let out an ugly word. And I'm as sure as can be in my heart he's innocent all the time. Sven, he's far and away above the rest of the children as the sun and the moon, and it's in my mind he's fretting for nothing at all. Ung-Joel might have done what they say, but never Sven."

Day after day Mor Elversson talked in the same strain. As soon as she and her husband were together, she would fall to praising Sven.

"You don't understand him, Joel," she would say. "And his ways, and how he's different. But I'd have thought you might have seen it by the difference in me. Washing and doing my hair neat, and sweeping and scrubbing and cleaning about the place. You don't suppose it's for your sake I do it?"

"Why," said Joel, "as for that, you've always been a great one for keeping things clean and neat beyond other folks." It was a way Joel had, of saying nice things to people whenever he could.

"It's not only that," said his wife, "but it's changed me in other ways. I'm never angry about things now — I've turned soft as an eiderdown. Did you ever see a smile like Sven's? When other folks look kindly at me, I'm glad enough, but when Sven looks at me that smiling way of his, I just feel I could fling myself naked into the sea if he said the word."

Joel laughed.

"I don't see there'd be any great gain in that if he did," he said. "But there's something in what you say there. To my mind, the boy's like one of the stones that lie down on the shore, and always being rolled about by the waves. He's got worn and smooth from all the hard knocks he's got, till there's not a sharp edge nor a corner anywhere."

Truth to tell, Joel, was at least as interested in his son as was his wife. But, pleased though he was with the lad, he could not but be anxious about him. It seemed as if he were resigned now, to submit to the judgment that had been passed upon him, and keep away from his kind for ever. There seemed little chance of his leaving the island. But even there, he would not be cut off from all communication with his fellows, unless he wished it so. Joel had been clerk to the magistrate's court for thirty years past, and in the course of that time had gained much knowledge of laws and regulations. In consequence, his help was often sought by neighbours wishing to make a will, draw up a contract, or arrange some similar matter in proper order. But when such visitors appeared, Sven Elversson never came in for a word with them. On the contrary, he would go off to the farthest part of the island as soon as a boat came in sight.

"Well, what's he to do?" said Mor Elversson, when her husband spoke of his anxiety. "To begin with, he's almost forgotten to speak his own tongue in all these years, and it's only just beginning to come back to him. And when folk themselves turn shy of him as if he was a monster, what's he to do?"

Joel threw back his head, drew in his breath audibly, and uttered words that his wife found it hard to understand.

"If I'd been born to be a musician," he said, "I doubt but I'd manage to find me something to play on."

"Well, and what then?" said his wife. "What do you mean by that?"

"I mean that, if it's as I think, and our Sven's meant to be a picture and example and show the way to others, then it can't be right for him to live here on this bit of an island like a hermit."

Mor Elversson looked at her husband, and a wealth of tenderness shone in her eyes.

"*You've* lived on this bit of an island all your life," she said. "But there's folk enough have been able to come and learn from you and plague you with no end of things."

Joel waved his hand impatiently.

"What's that compared to Sven? I never learned things when I was young, but Sven—he was set to it in time. There's nothing to stand in his way."

"There's one thing...."

"There's that, of course...."

"And that's everywhere, where you'd least expect it. Like a cat lying in wait, and before you know, it's at his throat."

"Ay," said Joel. "That's just the trouble. And what's done can't be undone. There's no sort of miracle could keep that cat from flying at him."

"But, Joel, remember, if it hadn't been for the trouble, he'd never have come back home to us again. Though I know in my heart he's innocent," she added.

And again and again she said the same. So overjoyed was she at having her son back home that she could hardly understand why he and his father troubled themselves about what other folk thought. "Never heed them," she said to Sven. "They're just foolish. You're better than all of them. The one that sneered at you the other day when you went to the post, he'd be in prison for forgery if he had his due. Don't fancy he's any call to look down on others."

But as time went on, she could not but feel that Joel was right, and that her son was gradually becoming a recluse, shunning his fellows altogether. And not only that. His manner had grown so humble that it almost made him appear ridiculous. He seemed wishful to efface himself altogether in his misery.

"No," she thought to herself. "This will never do. Something must happen soon. Surely the Lord will not forsake us altogether."

The parish of Applum, to which Grimön belonged, included, not only the level tract of the mainland as seen from the church, but also some dozen little islets off the coast, and the fishing village of Knapefiord, which last, with its boathouses and sheds, long quays and harbour basins, vessels and buoys, seems to spread out as far over the water as over the land.

Mor Elversson often rowed over to the village with butter and eggs, and in talking with her customers, housewives who had known her for years, she made frequent endeavours to praise this son of hers who had come home, assuring all that he could never have done any wrong.

But she soon found that all her pains were to no purpose. No unkind words were said, but those she spoke to pretended not to hear, as when a person known to be otherwise sensible enough makes some unreasonable assertion.

"Oh, they're over good and holy for this earth," said Mor Elversson bitterly, when she came home. "Full to the brim with faith and righteousness, till there's no room for a drop of mercy in them."

Joel himself met with no better success.

Of late, when people came to ask his help in this or that, he had taken to hinting that he was getting too old for the work, and that his son Sven ought soon to take over in his father's stead. But the suggestion passed unheeded everywhere. Fisher or farmer, whoever it might be, all were as deaf on that one subject as the sternly righteous housewives of Knapefiord.

On Christmas Eve, Joel and his wife and their son sat in the little dwelling at Grimön, talking of the future.

"Look here. Mother," said Sven, who seemed in particularly good humour this evening, "don't you think this kitchen place is dark and uncomfortable? What do you say to moving into the house itself?"

"Heavens!" cried his mother. "What's the boy thinking of! Why, there's neither roof nor floor to the place."

"That's no worse than can be mended," answered Sven. "I've been looking at the walls; they're sound enough. There's fine big rooms there, with plenty of light, and looking out over the sea. It's a shame to let the old captains' house go to rack and ruin."

Both father and mother agreed in this. But there was the question of money.

Sven explained that he had money of his own—not from his foster-parents, but money he had fairly earned. Before starting out on the expedition he had been promised a thousand pounds to be paid on his return. And this he had now received.

But Joel, for all that he had felt no qualms himself, suddenly saw how the old sea-captains who had lived there before would turn in their graves.

"Not with that money!" he cried. "I'd be glad to see the old house set to rights—but not with that money—no!"

Mother and son looked up at him in surprise. But both of them realized in a moment what was in his mind, and no more was said.

Joel sat thinking of the old sea-captains with their weather-beaten faces, their tarry fists and thirsty throats, good-natured, cheery men, not over-careful of their speech, nor dainty in their choice of company. His fathers, no doubt, had been of the same breed—and now he had told his son he was not good enough to live in the house that had been theirs. Told him that the money he had earned at the risk of his life on those same waters where they had voyaged and won their own was not good enough to be spent in mending their home.

There was a strange smile on Sven Elversson's face that evening—a gentle, patient, and forgiving smile. It had been there many a time before, when he had felt how his fellow men shunned him. But now, now that his father had shown a trace of the same feeling as all others had toward him, the smile of resignation seemed to settle on his face as if for good.

When Joel saw that look in his son's face, and marked how it stayed, and did not pass, he rose to his feet, and tried with kindly words to make amends. The boy answered with kindly words in return, but the look on his face remained.

Joel was angry with himself for having reopened the old wound. He understood that the lad had been keeping the news of the money a secret, in order to bring it out that very evening. And the sense of shame grew on him, till he felt unable to stay in the room, and took his hat and went out into the dark. Perhaps in his absence the boy's mother could tell him what were his father's real feeling toward him.

Hardly had Joel gone out, however, when a party of seven wild, drunken fellows came storming into the kitchen. They wanted Sven—Sven Elversson—to come out with them and be merry. They had taken a boat across on purpose to fetch him.

Mor Elversson looked at the men, and saw they were a crew of fishermen numbering some of the worst an wildest men on that part of the coast. And behind the rest, as if trying to remain unperceived, was one of her own sons, Ung-Joel, who was working in a store at Knapefiord.

And, turning from the drunken men with their unsteady gestures and foolish laughter, she looked at the boy, her son, whom they had come to plague and torture. A slender lad, finely built, with soft, gentle eyes and clean white hands. Neatly dressed he was, too, and shaved and orderly. He did not drink or smoke or spit about the place, and never a rough word passed his lips.

The others, who had come to make a jest of one in trouble, knew well enough that he had had a better upbringing than themselves, that he had led a richer life, and had a better understanding. They came because they hated him, because they looked on him as a worm to be trodden underfoot, a despicable creature that should not be let live in any Christian house.

As the strangers entered, a feeling of helplessness came over Sven. Not an ordinary faintness or loss of consciousness: it was simply that he felt unable to move. It seemed as if something were telling him plainly that this must be the end of his life. These men were come to torture him to death. And it was useless to resist. After all, life, as it was for him, now was hardly worth any great effort to preserve.

One of the men had found a dead snake by the roadside earlier in the day. He had taken it home and shown it to his comrades.

"Looks tempting," one of them had said.

"Yes. Anybody like to eat it?"

"Take it over to Grimön and ask Sven Elversson if he'd like it. He eats all sorts of things."

"Ay, just the thing for him."

And thus it was they had hit on the idea of coming to Grimön. They had a vague feeling that a man so vile as this Sven Elversson ought not to be left to enjoy his Christmas in peace; surely that was the very time he should be punished, and without mercy.

They had brought his brother with them to show them the way in the dark; the boy had agreed without any great reluctance. He was by no means as drunk as the others, but his feelings toward Sven were much the same as theirs. He was constantly being sneered at on account of the relationship, and many an ugly word was flung at him for his brother's misdeed. And he asked himself, what right had Sven to come home in this way and make trouble for them all? He stood now behind the broad backs of the rest, chuckling already at what was to come.

"Joel, Ung-Joel," cried his mother at sight of him. "What's all this? What do they want with Sven?"

The boy was used to answering without hesitation when that voice questioned him. And he spoke out now:

"They want him to eat a snake."

Sven Elversson felt even more powerless than before. He could see the whole scene; these men commanding him to eat, and he would refuse. Then they would set on him, with blows and kicks. And still he would say no. There was no power on earth now that could compel him to such a ghastly act—they might torture him to death.

But there was still a little respite left before he would be forced to go with them.

The fellow who had found the snake that morning drew out the long smooth thing from his pocket, and, rocking unsteadily, held it out before the mother's face.

"A rare little feast it'll be for him," he said.

"You call yourselves men?" cried the woman. "And you think I'll let him go with you, that's better than all of you together?"

The men burst out into a shout of laughter.

"He won't have to go farther than down to the shore," said the man who had just spoken. "We'll make a fire and cook it for him there."

Sven Elversson felt his strength returning. "It will soon be time," he said to himself. "By to-night it will be all over. And better so."

His mother glanced toward him, and marked how he sat still, with the same sad, forgiving smile on his lips. No trace of anger or sign of resistance showed in his face; only a gentle, submissive sadness.

"Sven, you're never thinking of going with them?" cried his mother. "D'you know who he is, that man there? Olaus from Fårön, that helped to kill his newborn child—and left the woman to bear it all when she'd most need of him."

The men roared with laughter.

"Don't be afraid, Mor Thala," said Olaus. "We'll look after Sven all right. We'll salt and pepper it for him and make it nice. A snake's nothing to him after what he's been used to."

"Look there!" cried the mother again, pointing to the biggest and wildest-looking of the men. "That's Corfitzson from Fiskebäck. He's done a power of evil in his day—and 'twas him that set fire to a shed full of cattle, to get the insurance money."

"Never mind her talk, boy, you come along with us," said Corfitzson, laying a hand on Sven's shoulder.

But Mor Thala went on without a stop.

"And there's Bertil from Strömsundet. If you'd know the worst of him, he's only starved his grandmother to death. She lived just two months after he came into the house. And him there in the corner—that's Torsson from Iggenäs, that never sold a fish but what he stole from others' nets, and those two there that can hardly stand for the drink in them, that's Rasmussen and Hjelmfeldt. They drink up all their earnings and leave their wives and bairns to starve."

Her voice had risen almost to a shriek; she was quivering with rage and terror. Even the men shrank back a moment before her fury, and forgot to laugh.

"And that one there, behind all the rest," she went on, bitterly. "Can you see who that is? Your own brother, Ung-Joel, it is. He's done no more harm as yet than leaving his father and mother to perish for lack of a helping hand. The times I've begged and prayed of him to come out here and help us, but he'd never hear. There, lad, that's the men that have come to bid you go with them—but you won't; you can't...."

But as she spoke, Sven rose to his feet, gentle and forgiving as ever, ready to submit and suffer.

The men laughed again.

"That's right, my son," said Olaus, who was evidently the leader. "Just as well to come with a good grace. You'd have little chance against the lot of us."

But Mor Elversson was not the one to give up without doing all in her power. With a rapid movement she grasped the body of the snake that Olaus still held in his hand, wrested it from him, and flung it into the next room, placing herself before the door.

At that moment the outer door opened, and Joel came hurrying in.

"What's here?" he said, looking round. "What are you rioting here about? What do you want with Sven?"

Two of the men had sprung forward to force Mor Thala aside from the doorway; two of the others had gripped Sven by the shoulders and were thrusting him before them.

Without a moment's hesitation the old man flung himself upon them.

"Out with you! Leave the boy alone," he cried.

And suddenly Sven Elversson was himself again. Something within him was whispering: "Now, now is the time! Father and mother are fighting on your side."

"Ung-Joel," he cried to his brother, who was still keeping away behind the rest. "Open the door there, quick!"

The boy obeyed instinctively; it was as if he could not disregard an order given in that house. In a moment Sven had gripped Olaus by the middle, lifted him off his feet, and flung him out.

Corfitzson rushed forward to the rescue, but found himself gripped in turn by a pair of strong arms, lifted, and flung out after his leader.

Then it was that Ung-Joel stepped forward and stood by his brother's side. There was a moment of wild tumult, and the place was cleared.

Ung-Joel bolted the door behind his former comrades. Then, solemnly, he stepped up to his brother and offered his hand.

"How did you manage it?" he asked, after a pause, with frank admiration. "I'll get you to teach me that throw."

The elder brother's face was flushed with the fight; his look of patient resignation was gone.

"You've given them a lesson, you may be sure," went on the younger. "They'll know better than to trouble you again. But what made you take it so patiently all this time, when you're a match for the worst of them?"

Now for the first time Sven Elversson lost his self-control. Sinking down in a chair, he buried his face in his hands.

"What's the use?" he cried, desperately. "How can I defend myself when all the time I hate myself more than any of them can ever do? Hate and loathe myself worse than you can ever think. Horrible, horrible. No one knows as well as I do what it is I've done—what it is I've sinned against. Is it any comfort to me to stop the mouths of a drunken crowd when all the time I've that on my mind that's ghastlier than all?"

THE "NAIAD"

A FEW days after Christmas, Ung-Joel came back to Grimön with a message from Olaus, to ask if Sven would take a share in the herring fishery on board the motor-boat *Naiad*, belonging to his crew.

"He says it's hardly likely you could get taken on with any other crew," said Ung-Joel; "but seeing that you're my brother, I was to tell you. They'll not be the best of company, I doubt, that sail with Olaus."

Mor Elversson declared at once that it was out of the question; Sven should never have any dealings with any of them. But his father thought otherwise.

"It wouldn't be a bad thing, perhaps, if Sven tried to pick up the ways of the fishery on the coast here," he said. "And it's true enough he'd hardly get taken on with any other crew."

"Joel! How can you talk so!" cried his wife. "Who knows what they've been plotting and planning now, to send for him like that. Some new mischief, I'll be bound."

"Why, I only said 'twas a pity Sven shouldn't have a part in the fishery," said Joel, mildly.

But Sven remembered his father's words on Christmas Eve, and it came into his mind now that perhaps it was his wish to get him away from home.

"You can tell Olaus I'll come," he said to his brother.

"And thank him for offering. I'll go over to Fårön myself as soon as I can."

"Why not come back with me now?" said Ung-Joel. "Then you can get the things you want at our store. There was a telegram in this morning that the herring are shoaling thick up at Smögen. By to-morrow they'll be getting away all about."

There was a hurry of preparation for a while, and then the two brothers set off, leaving Joel and Thala alone.

For a week or so they heard no news of Sven, then one Sunday Ung-Joel came out to visit them.

Mor Thala was eager to know how matters had gone with Sven and the crew—for all she knew, they might have killed him.

"I've heard nothing but what folk say," answered the boy. "And that's this. The crew of the *Naiad* before counted one man that had helped to kill a child, and one that had starved an old woman to death, one that had burnt down a place, and one that never sold but what he'd stolen, and two that were fast drinking themselves to death—and now they'd got another to help, and that a man who'd eaten human flesh, so it would be hard to find a rougher crowd on one keel. I've heard nothing from Sven himself, but, from all accounts, he seems to be getting on all right with them."

"That's foolishness," said his mother. But for all her angry looks, she was glad to learn that no ill had come to Sven. "But don't forget as soon as you've word from Sven to come here and let us know. 'Tis the best you can do for your father and me."

A fortnight later, Ung-Joel came out to the island again.

"Here's what they're saying now," he began. "That the *Naiad* men won't be able to stand much more of Sven. They say, here's the dirtiest, meanest, stinking little boat all along the coast getting gradually clean and workmanlike, the motor taken to working properly instead of going on strike when it's most needed, the rags of sails they used to help now and then been patched and put in order, the faded old flag done away with and a bright new one in its place and the name painted clean on the stern with all the letters in gold; the food on board getting that decent you wouldn't know but what you were on shore, and clean pots and pans in the galley. And the way folk look at it is this: the *Naiad* men, they might at a pinch take any sort of scoundrel on board, but clean pots and pans and all the rest, it's more than they can put up with."

"Ah! you're making fun of me," said his mother. But it was plain to see that she was glad at heart. "And don't forget," she went on, "as soon as you've any word from Sven, come out and let us know. He's done no wrong, and we must know how it is with him, that he doesn't come to any harm."

But folk that live at Grimön have need of all their patience, waiting for news. All through another two weeks Mor Thala waited, before Ung-Joel came with news of his brother.

"I haven't seen him myself yet," he explained. "But I've heard what they say, that it can't be long now before there's an end of it with Sven Elversson and the *Naiad* crew. It seems that Olaus—he's the skipper—has taken to seeing the men come on board to time, and more than once he's got his boat away with the rest of the fleet, instead of after, and got up in good time to the fishing grounds and made a fair haul. And what with the nets being sound and whole, instead of torn in parts and rotten the rest; when they bring up full catches, and the man at the windlass isn't dead drunk and tips the whole lot into the water alongside; when they're beginning to earn good money on the *Naiad*, why, it's plain that Olaus from Fårön and Corfitzson from Fiskebäck and Bertil from Strömsundet and Torsson from Iggenäs and Rasmussen and Helmfeldt won't stay long on board. They might bear with a man that's eaten human flesh, but to sail on a well-found ship and make good hauls like all the other crews, and earn good money—it's more than any of them have ever done before."

Mor Thala scolded him roundly for a fool that could never so much as speak one serious word, but she was pleased enough at the news he brought.

"You wait and see, it'll all be well yet," she said. "Eh, Joel, Joel—I wasn't meaning you, lad, but your father. He's surely the wisest man in all Bohuslän. He knew what he was doing when he let Sven go and take a share in that boat, he did."

A week or so later, Ung-Joel came in with a new report.

"I've not seen Sven myself," he said, "for the herring are keeping away up to the north this year. But I've heard what folk say. That when Olaus from Fårön goes spending money he's earned on doing up his house on shore, and Corfitzson from Fiskebäck puts his in the bank, as soon as it's paid him, and Bertil gets his wife a new dress, and Torsson buys a new boat, and Rasmussen and Hjelmfeldt start bringing home food for their wives and little ones—why, there must be something wrong with the *Naiad* lot somewhere. They might take a man-eater with them on board and nothing surprising in that, but to see them now with a clean ship and decently at work and living almost like honest folk, it's more than any'd believe."

"I never heard your like for talking wicked nonsense," said Mor Thala, but she was happier than she cared to show. And she declared that all would go well with Sven in the end; folk would come to look at him differently before long.

"The trouble is," said Joel, "that folk have always looked on that one thing one way, and it's hard for any to see differently. And it won't be easy for him to win them. We must be thankful if we can but see that it's not too much for the lad himself."

A week or so later, the two brothers came sailing home to Grimön together. They looked ill at ease as they entered the house.

Neither mother nor father ventured to question Sven, but Mor Thala soon managed to get Ung-Joel by himself.

"Now what's happened?" she asked.

"Ay, what's happened," said Ung-Joel, bitterly. "Little use that Olaus and Corfitzson and all the rest of them have turned better than they've ever been before, and can boast of a clean ship and a good season and a fine price for their fish, and the money well looked after, when they can't set foot in their own house but they're met by crying womenfolk. What's a man to do, when his own wife comes and begs and prays him and says better go on in the old way, bad as it was, than work and share with one that's done dreadful things like Sven. Says a man can't go near one that's done things like that without getting such himself that none can bear the sight of him after. Houses put to rights and boats and dresses and food and decency and comfort—they'd give it all and gladly, to be free of the one ugly thought. When things turn that way, what can a man do but go to Sven himself and beg of him to take off his hand from off the ship and crew, and say he'd better go back to Grimön and stay there, where there's none that's likely to meet him and be the worse for it."

THE SCHOOLHOUSE

THAT spring, soon after Sven had come back from the herring fishery, old Joel Elversson was asked by the Priest at Applum if he would care to undertake the building of the new schoolhouse.

Joel had done a good deal of building work before in the parish, and so cheaply that he had made but little for himself. And this was perhaps the reason why he was chosen now, though many might well have thought him too old for the work.

As soon as Mor Thala heard of the proposal, she at once declared that Joel was no longer able to undertake work of such responsibility, and her husband did not altogether oppose her view. But he pointed out that it would be hard if the parish were forced to get in a stranger for the work. And he himself would gladly have had some share in building a new school for the children, who had for long had to put up with the old and dark and draughty building that served at present.

"You should see the plans," he said to Mor Thala. "The things they hit on nowadays to make all fine and easy. They'd no such contrivances in my young days."

"You're set on that building work yourself, that's plain to see," said his wife. "It's my belief you've promised to take it on already."

The old man looked embarrassed.

"I'd not have done it if it wasn't that I'd a grown son in the house," he said.

"But surely you should have asked him first," said his wife. So much foresight and sharpness on the part of her husband was a surprise to her. Sven had been going about for some days looking moody and depressed; it seemed impossible to get him to undertake any work at all.

"I don't think Sven would regret it if he did take to building work," said Joel. "A man that's to live in his own house ought to know a bit about timber and foundations and the like. But if he won't help me. I'll have to say I can't do it after all."

It was a strange thing to her that her husband should ever think of getting Sven to work on a building connected with the Church, in a place where the general ill-will against him seemed stronger than anywhere else.

Sven was present when they talked it over, but said nothing at first. He knew well enough what was in his father's mind; it was his one idea and aim to get him to move about among folk. As to the failure of the *Naiad* cruise, Joel had merely said it had turned out far better than could be expected, and he had nothing but praise for his son. Sven himself had still but one desire, to hide himself away at home, but he felt now that his father would not permit him, until he had seen once more how impossible it was for his fellow men to forget the feeling of abhorrence with which they regarded him.

"I don't think Father ought to give it up now," he said. "I'll lend a hand gladly as far as I'm able."

Joel was highly pleased at this, and that very day he took Sven with him to make a round of visits to the others concerned: merchants, carpenters, masons, and workmen.

Almost against his will, Sven Elversson soon found himself keenly interested in the building, and his father let him take the lead. He was allowed to superintend the work, and to determine how it should be done. Grimön lies some distance from the mainland, and Sven did not care to waste so much time in journeys backward and forward, but lived close to the site while the work was in progress. Joel himself also began to tire of the everlasting trips from the island in to Applum, and for several weeks he stayed at home, leaving his son to take entire charge.

Whenever he went in to see how things were going, he invariably returned well pleased. His wife asked anxiously each time if there had been no expression of dissatisfaction among the Applum folk at Sven's taking over charge, but Joel was always able to reassure her.

"I met Israel Jonsson yesterday," he said, "the head of the council, and I asked him what he thought of the new schoolhouse. 'Well, Joel,' he said, 'I won't deny that we Applum folk were in two minds at first about getting your boy take over the work. But I think I can say now that both the school council and the parish council and all the rest would think twice about giving it elsewhere. When we see how he puts in granite under blocks instead of common stone, as it was thought, and find him building the walls of heavy timber, instead of thin planks that the architect thought would do, why, if there's any that bear him ill-will, they'd better put it in their pockets and do the sensible thing.'"

Mor Elversson began to understand now that Joel had accepted the contract solely and entirely in order to give Sven a chance of proving his worth and making friends. It was a kindly thought, she was forced to admit, but she was less confident now, and dared not believe it would succeed.

Next time Joel came back from the building site, her first question was whether Sven was still getting on, and if he had had no trouble with any of the people there.

"I'll not tell you what I think myself," answered Joel, "for you might not believe me. But I'll tell you word for word what Gunnar Markusson, that lives close by, said to me yesterday when I met him on the round:

"'I'll admit, Joel,' he says, 'that we were a bit uneasy in the parish about letting Sven Elversson take charge and build the new schoolhouse. But I will say now that, to my mind, the ratepayers would do well not to let their feelings run away with them, when it's a case of a public benefactor like Sven. He's putting in smoothed boards now, where we'd agreed we'd have to be content with unplanned wood. And he's using better paint than we'd reckoned on. He's roofing with tiles, instead of the tarred felt that was all we thought we could run to. And instead of cement steps at the entrance, he's making stone. It's this way with that boy of yours, that he'll have nothing but first-class work, and for all that it seems he's asking no more for the building than if he'd followed the plans from the first.'"

Mor Thala was overjoyed to hear that her boy was doing so well, but she felt nevertheless that the dreadful thing which haunted him was not to be so easily overcome.

Joel did not go over to the mainland again until September. He was away for several days, and when he returned, he brought Sven with him, and the news that the place was finished. The schoolhouse was built, and the inspection had taken place; the inspector could hardly find words to say how pleased he was with the result.

Mor Thala agreed that so far all was well. And, looking at her son, she felt that he looked like one released, from prison; she understood that he felt he had regained some little of the honour and respect he had lost.

And she was loth to spoil his pleasure, but as soon as she was alone with Joel, she asked if there really had been no one in all Applum who had made Sven feel he was not good enough for the work.

"There's none can say what folk think in their own minds," said Joel; "but I'll just tell you what the schoolmaster himself said to me yesterday, when I spoke to him after the opening.

"'There's no trusting to folk's gratitude,' he said, 'but if I was one of those whose children are to get their schooling in this new place, I'd show no unkindness to the man that built it. When you look at the hall there, the way he's chosen the best colours, and the neat and sound benches he's put up, the fine glass in the windows, well, it's a wonder how he could do it. And then all the fixtures in the *slöid* room, and the kitchen, and heating pipes, and gymnasium fittings and all—it's plain 'twas a lover of children that settled it all. There's many might well wish to be children again just to go to school in the place Sven Elversson's built.'"

Mor Thala could not but be pleased at this, and was glad now to feel that all her anxiety had been unfounded.

THE STONEHILLS

SVEN ELVERSSON had been in to Göteborg to settle some accounts for building materials supplied for the schoolhouse, and came back by train. On arrival at the station nearest Applum, he found that the conveyance which was to have met him there had not come.

It was over ten miles to walk, and he stood in the station puzzling how he was to get back, when a small carriage with two horses drove up and stopped. It was from the inn at Applum, and, on inquiry, Sven learned that it had been ordered by the Priest, who had just married a clergyman's daughter from a distance, far away in Norrland.

Sven Elversson had likewise ordered a carriage from the inn, but it was now clear that his message had gone astray; no carriage had been sent for him. The driver suggested that he should ask the Priest to let him ride on the box, but Sven did not wish to push himself forward, and would not hear of it.

They were still discussing the question, when the Priest and his young wife came out from the station.

They made a handsome pair. The Priest, just over thirty, was a man of middle height, powerfully built, and with a splendid head. He wore a full beard, dark and curling; had a broad, handsome forehead, well-cut features, and fresh complexion, with white teeth. Altogether, he seemed all that a young girl could wish for; a man to cherish and protect her, work for her, and give her a good place in the world. The young wife, too, was surprisingly beautiful. Sven Elversson was reminded of the type so favoured by some English painters: handsome women with tall, slender figure and sloping shoulders, slightly bowed head, rich hair prettily shading the face, straight eyebrows and delicate cheeks, and with a look in the brilliant eyes that seemed looking out of a strange world toward heaven.

It struck him as curious that, as he watched the pair, the Priest seemed gradually to lose all that Sven had formerly found attractive in him. The fine, unspeakably delicate lines and colouring of the woman seemed to render the man coarse and mean, almost ugly, by comparison. And Sven hoped that he was not influenced by ill-feeling toward the Priest from the time of that scene in the church, in feeling now that this was but a poor husband for the slight, dainty creature at his side.

Sven Elversson moved quickly away as the two came up, but he heard the driver asking on his own account if he might take Sven with him on the box, whereupon the Priest came forward and invited him to drive with them.

The Priest had, indeed, always treated him with kindness, and now, as Sven Elversson sat on the box and the carriage drove off, he tried to efface the impression of a moment ago. "I was mistaken, as I often am," he said to himself. "I should say that I have not seen for years a pair so completely suited as these two. And well they may be. Here is the husband sitting and thinking how different life will be now in the little vicarage at Applum, with a young mistress to fill the place with life and gaiety—while she on her part is dreaming of all she will do to make the home so comfortable that he will never wish to leave it, and always be longing for it when he is away."

So completely had Sven surrendered himself to this view, that he was astonished when a little later the young wife exclaimed, in a tone of weariness, even impatience:

"Oh, will they never end?"

"What is it she wants to end?" thought Sven to himself. "What can it be that could trouble her this day of all days?"

Sven Elversson looked round on all sides. And suddenly he understood. It must be the stonehills.

It was indeed a strange-looking landscape they were driving through.

Mountain country one could not call it, for there were neither peaks nor mountain ridges; on the other hand, it was not a level plain, for the ground was broken everywhere by hillocks of rock, large and small. In places, they were so close together as hardly to leave a passage between; then they would lie farther apart, with broad open spaces large enough for homestead and field. Right and left, behind and before, the same—truly a stranger might well ask if they would never end. The road wound in and out between them, and never the crest of a hill so high that they could see across them, to what lay beyond. All along the way were stonehills, and ever more behind. Some were sparsely clad with a poor growth of grass, others were bare, and others again showed patches of bush and heather; save for this, they were all alike.

Now and again, an open space between led one to hope that the ground might be clear beyond, but one had scarcely time to frame the thought before a new hillock thrust itself into view.

"It must be different in Norrland, of course," thought Sven. "And these stonehills of ours are dark and forbidding enough, it is true. A pity they should be the first this little lady sees of Bohuslän."

And next moment he heard her telling her husband that she felt as hopelessly lost among these stony hills as in the darkest forest.

In one place a flock of sheep could be seen grazing, then a couple of cows, or again some children picking berries. And the young wife declared that it was well they were there, for had it not been for the sight of children and homely animals, she would hardly have believed they were in a Christian country.

"Sigrun, how can you say such a thing!" exclaimed her husband. "This is Bohuslän, my own country, and I love every stone and every tuft of heather in it. What would you have said if I had spoken so about the pine forests and the moors of Norrland?"

As was but natural, his words took effect. The young wife was silent at first for a while; then she whispered something, with tears in her voice, and Sven understood that she was begging her husband's forgiveness for having spoken so about his country.

"I'm not like that other days, really. I don't know what can be the matter with me to-day," she said.

Every word she uttered was a delight to hear; so solemnly and sincerely she spoke, with the slightest trace of a lisp in her voice. "God forbid she should be otherwise for my part," thought Sven. "Surely 'tis only beautiful that she should be afraid of all ugly things."

Nothing more was said for a time, but then the little lady began again, with a strange quiver in her voice:

"Edward, I know it's wrong of me to trouble you, but I can't help it. I am so afraid. I've been trying to overcome it by myself, but I can't—it won't go away. And then I just remembered that I shan't need to struggle against things all alone now—that I've you to help me with all my weakness."

There was such a depth of entreaty in her tone that Sven Elversson felt embarrassed at sitting there where he could hear. He felt himself unworthy even to over-hear the thoughts and feelings of this delicate lady.

She was trying now to explain to her husband that she was actually afraid. She fancied she had seen these hills somewhere before—had fled for her life among such a confusion of rocky hills, with some behind that sought to kill her. Or that there was someone even now lying in wait there, ready to fall upon them. Something terrible there must be, close at hand. She had but one desire, to get away from the place.

Her voice told that she was in greater fear even than she would admit, and that this was deadly earnest. Sven Elversson himself could not help smiling where he sat, and the Priest was utterly unable to understand her fear of nothing at all; he tried to answer gaily, and pass it over with a jest.

But his endeavours failed of their effect. She declared, with sudden violence, that if Applum were as cold and shut in as here, she could never live there.

"And it's wicked and wrong of me to say so, I know," she said; "but I've been thinking of it all the time, while we've been driving here; if I cannot find something beautiful at the end of it, something to help me, I shall be haunted by the same fear there as well. I shall be dreading every day that something terrible will happen."

Sven Elversson thought of the plain at Applum, with the vicarage behind the church, set in a little hollow to be sheltered from the wind. And he wondered if she would find any comfort in the evenly divided fields, the dark wall of hills all round, the narrow view, the homesteads painted blue and white and red, and the treeless meadowland.

"'Tis none so easy for him just now," thought Sven. "I'd find it hard myself to comfort her in his place. But he knows her, and loves her—it makes all the difference."

The Priest must have been thinking of the same thing. He sat for a while without speaking.

"Let me tell you of a dream I had last winter," he said at last. "It made me very happy at the time, that dream, and perhaps it may help you too.

"I dreamed that I was driving along the road to your home at Stenbroträsk, and it was toward the end of winter, bare earth and leafless trees, and the road a sodden stretch of mire. The bridges were out of repair, and the horse was a wretched beast that could hardly move at all.

"There was a keen, cold wind from the north, and everything was gray and dismal, and the few houses here and there along the way looked poor and miserable; the whole country seemed inhospitable and depressing.

"Then at last, coming up over the hill, I caught sight of the steep river-bank, and the church and the house at Stenbroträsk, and in a moment all was changed. The air seemed warmer, the fields were green, the birches wore a veil of leaf, the road was firm and good—everything was kindly and smiling as if in welcome; even the horse came suddenly to life and trotted on bravely.

"But the strange thing about it all was that I felt the spring and the warmth came from myself. They had not been there before, but now, as if by magic, they came—and all because of the warmth that filled my heart at sight of your home. And there seemed nothing strange about it all in my dream—it was all natural and as it should be."

Here the Priest paused, and his wife, in a changed voice, asked what happened after.

"There was no more," he answered. "For the warmth at my heart was so good to feel that I woke." And, having said this, he was silent again.

But those few words of love, the little glimpse of something beautiful, had filled the young wife's heart with joy, and the listener in front heard her whisper to her husband in a voice almost stifled with emotion:

"You mean that if I had but the same warmth in my heart as you, I should find beauty in this country of yours, and in your home—even in these dreadful hills."

And then gladly and confidently she went on:

"Do not be afraid for me. There is nothing to frighten me now. I feel now as you felt in your dream."

"There," thought Sven to himself. "See how little one can judge things at first sight. Truly she could not have found a better husband than Pastor Rhånge. He has a good heart and a good head. Who else could have answered her so well?"

THE SEA

THE newly married pair had come home on a Tuesday. On Saturday in the same week, Sven Elversson went up to the vicarage with some papers about the school. He walked straight up the front steps and through the hall into the office, and stopped just inside the door.

It was the Pastor's day for business, he knew, and though it was rather late, he had never thought but that he would find the Priest sitting at his writing-table. But he was not there—was not in the room at all. He could not be far away, however, for the big books that were always used on business days lay open on the table, and a pen was in the inkstand.

It was not Sven's way to push himself forward, and he did not care to go through to the kitchen and ask if the Pastor was at home, or look for him in any of the other rooms. There could be no harm, he thought, in staying where he was, to wait a little.

But as he stood, there was a sound of voices in the next room; the door was ajar, and he could hear every word distinctly.

"Sigrun"—it was the Pastor speaking, in an easy tone:—"the post ought to have been here by now. But I can't go down for it myself to-day, in case any one comes."

"Why, then," answered his wife cheerfully, "that's easily managed. Malin will be going down to the store directly, and she can bring back your paper at the same time."

Evidently the Pastor had only gone out for a moment to ask about the post, thought Sven. He would be back now, since that was settled.

But the Pastor spoke again.

"Well," he said, "don't you think now you might go yourself? Wouldn't you like a little walk? It's lovely out just now, and the road has dried after the rain of yesterday. It would do you good to get out in the air a little."

He spoke gently and kindly, as if thinking only for her good. And the young wife answered as kindly again.

"I'd go and gladly," she said, "but look at these curtains strewn all about the room. I can't go till I've got them up."

There was no more to be said after that, thought Sven. But he noticed at the same time how the Priest's voice, manly and strong in itself, seemed to lose its pleasant tone, and become rough and coarse, when heard beside his wife's soft, gentle speech.

And it seemed that the matter was not ended yet, after all, as he had hoped. The Priest began again.

"Oh, of course, one couldn't expect a great lady like yourself to go and fetch a paper for her husband," he said. This must be meant in jest, surely. But it sounded at the same as if he were annoyed at her refusing to do as he wished.

"Oh, Edward, you know it's not that."

"Or perhaps Applum's too dull and ugly a place for you to care to go out at all. Her ladyship doesn't care to take the air unless there are fine houses and big estates all round. Perhaps I had better order the carriage, so that——"

"Edward!" she cried.

"Oh, I know there's nothing here to compare with your own place," he went on, with a little ill-tempered laugh. "But I didn't think you were too proud to set foot to the ground in Applum, for all that."

"Edward, it isn't that at all. I can't go just now."

"You *can't* go?" asked her husband, with an air of profound astonishment.

All this had passed before Sven had time to think. "I ought not to hear," he said to himself. And to make his presence known, he rattled the handle of the door, opened the door itself and closed it again, stamped his feet and coughed. But no one seemed to notice, and the two in the next room went on again.

"No, I can't," repeated the young wife. "There is something in this place that stifles me; I can't breathe. It isn't just longing for home, but something more. I am well and happy enough as long as I keep to the house, but as soon as I go out it comes over me again."

She spoke passionately, flinging out her words in broken snatches.

"But, Sigrun," said the Priest, "what is the matter with you? I meant no harm."

"I'm not so proud, indeed I'm not," she cried. "Ask any of those at home, and they'll tell you it was never my way to be so. And it's not because the place is not pretty to look at that I can't bear to go out. No, it is something else—if only I knew what it was!"

"Look here, Sigrun," said her husband, "you must tell me what all this means. We must talk this over seriously, that's clear."

Sven Elversson was at a loss to know what to do. He had already heard too much, perhaps; it would make matters worse to let them know he had been there. He walked to the door, but turned back again. He was always in doubt now as to how to act. It would be hard to find a man so undecided and lacking in self-confidence.

"I didn't want to tell you about it," said the young wife, speaking breathlessly and impatiently as before, "for I know it's nothing really. Only something that comes over me as soon as I go outside the house. Not anything I can see or hear, but something that makes me feel miserable and sorry for myself. It is cruel to think that I must go about here always, and never get away; I feel as if I had been condemned for some crime. It is just that—to feel myself condemned to stay for ever in one place, the same little, narrow, monotonous, cheerless place."

"Now I know," thought Sven to himself, "she is only saying this so that he shall say something beautiful in return, as he did before. And the Priest's a man with the heart and head to set her right again—'twill be easy enough for him."

"Oh, if only one could look out and see far away—if only I were not buried here, in a hole, and had not that wall of hills all round. But it must be a punishment for something I have done, or I should not have come here. Oh, can't you say something to help me?"

Now it must come, thought Sven. Now surely he would say some beautiful thing. And it would be fine to see how he would help her again this time.

Truth to tell, Sven Elversson was perhaps not sorry to be standing where he could hear all this. The young wife's voice was very sweet. And he was sure the Priest would say something wonderful now; something inspiring and good to hear.

"I have tried again and again," she went on, "to go out. But I can't. You can't think what it is like. I feel as if I were choking; I feel it here in my throat. And I've cried——"

"But there is nothing," said the Pastor. "Surely, Sigrun, you must know that. There is nothing in the air here that we cannot see. It is all imagination."

"There *is*! There is something here—I can feel it. Something that hates me, and is trying to take away my happiness. Do you know what I have been doing lately? I go and look at that poor little picture of Stenbroträsk, that one of my cousins did for me—I laughed at it then. But now, when I have looked at it a little, the river and the house and the big rowan trees by the gate, it seems to give me courage enough to go on living."

"I am afraid, my dear, you are giving way to a foolish fancy," said her husband. And the listener marked how he slipped into the admonitory tone of the preacher. "You must really try to overcome it before it has gone too far. And I think, really, I must ask you now to go and do as I said—go down to the post at once."

"But I can't!" she cried. "I can't—I can't!"

Sven Elversson knew, of course, that the Pastor was honestly acting for the best. But—he had thought he would have found some other way. Still, perhaps after all this was best. He himself would hardly have known what to do.

"Listen to me, Sigrun," said the Priest. "You must surely understand that it is childish to give way to such ideas. The only thing to do is to overcome it. You are well and strong; you will not tell me that you cannot walk that little way. Anyhow, I must ask it of you, for the sake of our happiness—if you wish it to last for life, and not for a few weeks' honeymoon only."

"I will go another time," she said, humbly, despairingly. "But—won't you let me off for to-day? I will try in a day or two; I will try to-morrow."

Sven Elversson stood listening yet a moment, anxious to hear if the request would be granted. But when the Pastor repeated that he must have his paper now, at once, Sven saw in a flash what he should have done before, but in his confusion had not thought of. Very quietly he opened the door and slipped out. He walked slowly until out of sight of the vicarage, and then set off at a run down to the post.

And so, when the young wife came walking slowly, so slowly, down the road, with tears on her eyelashes after what had passed, and trembling, half-unconscious, as if she had risen from a sick-bed, she had not to go many steps before a young man stepped up to meet her.

He greeted her politely, and said something about having driven with them from the station a few days back.

She made no answer, only stared at him, without understanding at first what he meant. He endeavoured to explain that he had been to the store; she fancied afterward he must have been going to say something about the storekeeper having asked him to take the paper up with him to the vicarage. He spoke softly, and with so much hesitation that she would have found it hard to understand him even had she been herself at the time.

He handed her a newspaper, which she took, but still she walked on, as if unable to realize that here was the thing she had been sent to fetch; that she could go back home now as soon as she pleased.

Then the young man came up to her again, saying something about going another way, if she wished to go for a walk. He begged her humbly to excuse him for the liberty, but seeing she was a stranger to the place, and a fine evening, if she would not rather go down and look at the sea.

In the midst of all her fear and trouble of mind, with the same stifling feeling at her throat, she caught a word of the sea, and stopped, and looked at him.

"The sea? Is there any sea near here?" she asked.

"Indeed there is," he answered. And if she were not above letting him show her the way, it would not take long to get there.

He turned off along a little path running straight toward the west, and she followed. She noted that he was dressed as a workman of the better class, and had a kindly, honest face, though his manner was strangely humble. She felt no hesitation about going with him now.

It was a beautiful evening, with a curious reddish light that seemed to float down from the sky. It was as if the air about her took colour, and became visible. She felt as if it were filled with tiny, delicate rose-leaves, that came falling softly down, like snowflakes, making the plain all round blush faintly, like a bride.

And when they came out toward the western hills, she saw that they did not make one continuous barrier, as she had thought. The wall consisted of huge masses of rock, but with passes leading through in many places.

The young workman led her out between the rocks, and on the farther side there was white sand on the ground, with here and there a shell. Then, after turning a corner of the cliffs, she stopped and drew a deep breath.

Before her was a broad, open expanse. All the rich red sea of air, and all the wide sea of water spreading out and away, with nothing to shut it in. Open, free, as far as the sun itself, that was sinking toward the western verge.

There was no land to be seen out there save a narrow strip of sand with a long stone mole, and, farther out, a few black reefs rising from the pearly water.

And at sight of all this, she felt in a moment that she was saved. For where could she choose to be rather than here, in a place with so much beauty, so near at hand—so much beauty that she could see every day.

How could it be that no one had ever told her of this? She sat down on a stone and rested there a long while, drinking in the light with her eyes. Her eyes wandered over the wide expanse, looking as far as they pleased, like birds released from a close cage.

And she thanked God for her home, and for the sea, so great and strong and clean, so near her.

She must have sat there long without speaking. When she looked up, the young workman had gone.

Truth to tell, she was pleased at this. She could always thank him, another time. It was pleasanter now to be alone.

She felt stronger now, and more hopeful—better able to fight against the stifling sense of something threatening that hung over the plain.

Suddenly she remembered her husband—he might be anxious about her. And she rose to go home, to tell him that she was better now, and happier. And to thank him for his sternness in sending her out to face her trouble boldly.

SAILING

IT WAS a Sunday morning in late October. A heavy wind came sweeping up from the south, from lands where the air was yet warm, where roses still budded and bloomed, where the vines were newly stripped, and the juice of the grape foamed in the presses.

The heavy south wind spoke with a strange, disquieting sound. Listening to it, one felt confused, as if hearing a stranger speak in some foreign tongue. Who could say what it was trying to tell—whether some great secret, or merely a whisper of all the yellowing trees, the fallen wings of butterflies, the empty nests, it had passed on its way?

That Sunday, Sven Elversson had come over in the boat to land his father at the little harbour outside the barrier rocks of Applum; the old man had gone in to service at the church. But Sven did not go with him; as soon as his father had gone, he sought out a cleft in the rocks a little to the right. It was a place he knew well; he had lain there often on the green heather as a child.

This was the happiest time Sven Elversson had known since his return. The patient, sorrowful smile had begun to fade from his lips, and the bitter trouble that had filled his soul no longer tortured him as before. And as he lay there on a ledge of rock, listening to the wind, wondering what it was trying to tell him, and staring out over the sea, he called to mind a vision he had seen one day, when he had been lying just as now on a rocky slope by the shore, with a broad expanse of sea spread out before him. The bright glitter of the sunlight on the water had tired his eyes, and he had lain quite still for a long time. Then, suddenly opening his eyes and glancing down at the great water, he had seen a mermaid.

It was only the briefest glimpse; she was gone the moment his eyes fell on her, changed to a fleck of white mist that floated away over the water.

But he had seen her—and the thought filled him with a great joy; he felt himself favoured, honoured beyond others, and supremely happy at having been granted a sight of one of those lovely spirits of nature that fill the air and sea, yet hide themselves so jealously from the sight of men.

He was certain that a whole flock of mermaids had been playing there on the shore, but had vanished the moment he sought to open his eyes. All but that one, who had not been able to escape in time.

He had never forgotten it, and since then he had never sat alone by a quiet sea but he must close his eyes and lie very still for a time, that the mermaids might think he slept, and venture out from the deep. But never since that once had he gained a glimpse of any.

To-day he tried again, though with little hope. And when he felt he had been quiet long enough, and opened his eyes, he started almost in dismay. True, there was no mermaid, no figure half maiden, half a fish, to be seen amid the waves. But there, on a tall rock just at the water's edge, sat a woman. A young, slender creature, clad in white, and seated with easy poise on top of the rock—she seemed as if she might as well have come there from the sea as from the land.

But it was soon plain to see that the woman sitting there was no joyous fairy being. She dried her eyes again and again with a handkerchief—after all, no more than a poor human creature, that could suffer and shed tears.

Sven Elversson sat watching her, wondering what it could be that troubled her. Was it more ugly stonehills again, more prisoning barriers of rock, that made her fear so that she could not go to church, but must sit alone and weep beside the sea?

He saw how her slight figure shook with sobs; her whole attitude told him that it was no light burden that weighed her down. And he understood that she had come to seek for comfort from the sea, having no other to whom she could turn. And this time the sea had not helped her.

A moment later the woman turned at a slight sound behind her. A man was clambering down the slope; she recognized him, surely, as the young workman who had shown her the sea here some weeks ago. Hastily she dried her eyes and went toward him; she had not thanked him yet.

"I saw you sitting there," said he, "and I thought, if I might be so bold ... I've my boat close by here, a good boat, though not much to look at. And if you'd honour me so far. I'd be very glad to take you for a sail."

Had it been any other day, she might not have accepted. But, just now, she felt so grateful for any little crumb of kindness that she could not refuse. And she did not wish that this young workman, who looked so modest and kind, should think she declined because he had only a common, workaday fishing-boat to offer her, and was himself but a common man in his working clothes. Though it was Sunday, Sven was wearing his heavy sea-boots and rough clothes, with a sou'wester that suited him well; it looked like the steel helmet of some old sea-king.

So they pushed off from land, and he hoisted the sail, and the heavy south wind filled it, sending the boat heeling to one side. Sven put the rudder hard over, heading due west, and the little vessel flew out across the bay toward the open sea.

Fru Rhånge had at first no thought of any pleasure to herself in going out for a sail to-day. She had not thought there was anything in the world that could make her forget the weight of sorrow that burdened her now. But when they had been sailing a little while, she could not help feeling easier; fresher in body and stronger in mind to bear her trouble.

The sky was clear, save for a few little flecks of white cloud. But there was yet enough moisture in the lower air to soften the light and tinge the dry, bare surface of rocks and reefs and islets with shades of grayish red and blue. They seemed, too, now to rise more boldly and strongly from the water, standing out with a certain majesty against the rest. The clefts seemed deep and black, the slopes steep and terrible and perilous; the distances seemed more marked, with ridge upon ridge in a succession of ever softer and more heavenly hues.

And after a little while there came into the young wife's eyes a look of quiet, earnest questioning, and she laid her folded hands in her lap as if in worship of all the beauty spread about her.

She was filled with a single thought—that she was learning to know one of God's miracles. She was learning to know the sea. She had never known before what it was to be so near the sea, to feel its breath in one's ears, to watch the play of expression in its face, to nestle close to its breast and be lulled to calm and peace.

Sven Elversson put the helm over, and they ran across to the north, in between the reefs, sailing close in under rugged cliffs, by little red fisher-huts set among ancient pear trees heavy with red-brown fruit, with glimpses of meadow between the rocks, greener, more brilliantly, livingly green than in the kindliest spring.

He led her from sound to sound, meeting white steamers, heavy, deep-laden barges, and lighter craft that glided over the water like huge sailing butterflies.

Sven Elversson himself looked at it all with something like amazement. Reef and islet, houses and meadows and trees—there was a greatness, a wealth of colour, a beauty over all to-day unlike other days. And he was glad that she had seen them thus, in their festal array.

They must have known, he thought to himself, how deeply this woman loved all that was beautiful.

And it was with Sven as with all the rest, the land and sea. He was seen at his best to-day.

They talked at first of the weather, and of all the beautiful things about them, and he taught her the names of all the rocks and islands as they passed. But after a while they came to speak of other things, of every possible thing, old things and new, as if they had been tried friends.

And he laid aside the barrier of humility and shyness, and spoke freely and naturally, until she wondered, and thought that young men born by the sea, and voyaging early abroad to other lands, must gain an education and experience beyond others who spent all their days on land.

She felt a real trust in him, for he was good and gentle and wise; she wished she knew him better, and had such a man to turn to when her own wits were at a loss.

As for Sven, he had not spoken with her long before there came over him an intense longing to tell her of his sin, to confess it all to this innocent creature who knew nothing of sin herself.

It crossed his mind that all those who had hitherto condemned and despised him were themselves well acquainted with sin and vice. All had no doubt at some time cheated, lied, stolen, borne false witness, been proud and merciless, idle, miserly, revengeful, or cruel.

But this young girl from a pious home had lived a quiet and protected life, untouched by passion or covetousness. She had as yet no knowledge of sinful nature, her own or others'. She had never cherished an evil thought, never wished harm to any soul.

He could not expect her to judge him over-leniently, for she was keenly sensitive, and could never control her abhorrence of all that was ugly and evil to her mind. But be that as it might, he would gladly submit to her judgment; she should be his court of appeal. He could not go to the King for justice, but he could go to her.

For some time, however, he refrained, shy and uncertain of himself. And while he sat hesitating, he noticed that she had grown silent again. She seemed to be trying to say something that was hard to begin.

At last, however, she made up her mind and came straight to the matter at once.

"You saw I was crying when you came up before?"

"Yes," he said. "I could not help seeing that."

"It wasn't anything very much," she said. "Only a letter that came. It was from a friend of mine, a rich man's daughter, just married, and her husband was such a good man, clever, and looked up to by everyone; we all thought she would be so happy."

"And now—you mean she is not?" Sven laid both hands on the tiller and leaned forward. He seemed keenly interested in all that concerned this friend of hers.

"No," she answered, looking out over the sea, as if seeking to avoid his glance. "She is not happy. She writes that her husband is always displeased with her somehow. And she can't understand it. She asked if I could tell her what it might be. But I can't. I would gladly help her, but I can't understand it myself. So you can understand I was sorry. That was why I couldn't help crying."

"Yes, I understand," Sven replied. "But your husband, lady. Pastor Rhånge is a man of great experience. Ought you not to ask him about it?"

Fru Rhånge coloured, and gave him a quick glance, almost of suspicion. But his eyes met hers frankly and openly, without a thought of anything to conceal, and she went on:

"I do not think she would like me to speak to my husband about it. It is always when they have been out anywhere and are driving home that he is—displeased with her. Hardly speaks to her at all. And whenever she tries to say anything, he only answers with an unkind word or a sneer."

"But are you sure there is not anything in her behaviour that could offend him? Anything wrong, I mean?"

"No," answered the young wife, eagerly. "That, I am certain, there is not. They are earnest-minded, both of them, and wherever they go, among friends, it is always quiet; no dancing or noisy games or anything like that. But she did think of that, too, that perhaps he found her too gay in her manner, and last time they were out she sat all the time with the old married women and talked sensibly. Only when the host came and wanted to show her the garden did she go out at all. And he was an elderly man, and they spoke of nothing but trees and flowers, and how there were not enough gardens round about. And she was so interested, and asked him if he did not think they could manage a little garden at her home. And he promised to send some of his own people over that autumn to mark out a garden for her, and then in the spring he would send her some things to plant in it. But then in the evening, driving home with her husband, she told him about it, and thought he would be pleased. But he gripped the whip so hard as he listened, she could see the knuckles grow white, and when the horse stumbled he was furious, and lashed it again and again. And he told her that their home would stay as it was, and as it had been, and he'd have no gardener people coming to alter this and that. And told her not to enter into any arrangements of that sort in future without first asking his permission. And she tells me now she was so frightened she could not say a word. Only folded her hands and prayed to God to show her what it all was, what it could mean."

The young wife spoke throughout very slowly, choosing her words with care, and Sven Elversson listened with growing interest. And he could not help thinking that the description of the old man who was so fond of gardens fitted in excellently with a landowner living a little way out of Applum, near the sea; he had a big place, and would naturally have invited the Pastor and his wife some time.

"She must be very pretty, I suppose—your friend," was all he said.

Again she cast a covert, searching glance at him.

"I daresay people would think her quite good-looking," she said, carelessly. "But what joy can it be to her, when her husband has so much to find fault with in all that she does? When it seems as if she were never to have her will in anything; and all that she cares to do is wrong? And never can learn what she may do and what not?"

Sven Elversson was getting the sail over ready to tack, and had not time to answer before she went on:

"Before, when she was at home, no one ever spoke unkindly to her for what she did. Everyone seemed pleased with her then. She was a good example to her little brothers and sisters, they said, and wondered how they would manage when she was gone. And whenever she thinks of that time she cannot help smiling at herself, for now that she has a home of her own, it seems she can do nothing right, and is scolded for all she says or does not say, whatever she does or does not do."

Sven Elversson was at a loss how to answer. "She is all alone," he thought, "and has no one to confide in; helpless and a stranger. And she needs someone to talk to; it helps her a little to talk of it this way."

And he said only that Fru Rhånge seemed to care very much for her friend.

"I wish I could help her," she said, and was very near to weeping again. "For I know she is good and kind, really. She loves to help and comfort old people, and the poor, when they are in trouble, but she must not do that now, and that is almost the worst thing of all. And she may not sit in the pew that belongs to her home in church, though she likes best to sit there, because it is just in the choir, and a little above the rest, so she can see out over the congregation."

Sven Elversson thought of the little pew in Applum church, set aside for the family of the incumbent; it stood a little higher than the others, and one had a view of the rest of the church from there. "But how can I tell her," he thought, "that her husband is jealous? It would only hurt her. Perhaps it will pass over. Better that she should not know."

He turned the vessel now, and made for home. It was as well that her husband should find her there when he came back from church.

And in his pain at not daring to help her—perhaps to turn her thoughts from her own trouble—he pointed to a rocky island far to the west.

"That is Grimön," he said. "That is where the fellow they call Sven Elversson lives. You've heard of him, maybe?"

She nodded. "Yes, I have heard about that—the whole story."

She seemed inclined to let the matter end there, but suddenly she added a few words that made an end of the little happiness Sven had felt that morning.

"You've heard, of course, that the schoolhouse he built over by the church was burnt down last night?"

"Burnt down!" he cried. And in consternation he loosed his hold of the tiller, so that the sail was flung over and the boat nearly capsized.

"Yes," said Fru Rhånge, with perfect calmness, "burnt down to the ground. And a good thing, too!"

Sven brought the boat round again. "Why do you say that?" he asked between clenched teeth. "Why is it a good thing the place was burnt? I have heard that the folk in Applum were pleased enough with the building."

"I have heard so, too," she said. "But what was the good of that when the children would not go there?"

"Children would not go there?" he repeated, helplessly. "I have not been over to the mainland since it started—I knew nothing of that."

Fru Rhånge could see he was astonished at her saying it was well the place was burnt, and she went on eagerly to explain. From the very first, the children had taken a dislike to the new school. They had heard it was built by a man who had eaten human flesh, and they feared they would lose all chance of salvation if they sat at their lessons in a place that smelt of Christian blood.

And, as she told all this, she wondered why the man before her sat there so quietly, as if unconscious, with a far-away look in his eyes and a patient, suffering smile on his lips.

And in order to justify what she had already said, she went on to relate how the schoolmaster and, most of all, the mistress in charge of the little ones, had done all they could. Had spoken kindly and sensibly to the children, shown them how well the new school was built and fitted, and how all had been thought out to make it useful and comfortable for them. But the children had no ears for that, and persisted all the same: the place had been built by a wicked man, a dreadful sinner, and it was unclean.

Some of them had suddenly begun to cry during the lessons. Others had fancied they saw visions, and the fear and horror grew day by day. At last the parents could hardly get their children to go at all; it was even feared that some of the more excitable would go out of their minds.

Sven Elversson sat looking straight before him. "I wished her to be my judge," he said to himself. "And so it has come about. She condemns me, like all the rest."

She went on to say that it was of the children she had been thinking when she had said it was a good thing the school had been burnt. The fire had been caused by a pure accident. The woman who came to clean the rooms had upset a lamp: the fire had spread at once, and before she could get help it was beyond control.

The man at the helm looked up. "Well, well," he said. "Now Sven Elversson has been judged by God and man. Now it will be said that God would not suffer such unclean hands to build a house for children."

"Really, it almost seems——" began the woman, and checked herself. By a sudden intuition she felt now that the fellow there, who had been in her company for two hours at least, must be Sven Elversson himself.

Had she not heard his name mentioned the first time, when he had driven with them from the station? She had not noticed it at the time. But now ...

She looked at him closely. His simple dress had deceived her; she could see now that his face was that of an educated man. And then the curious little accent that she had noticed and wondered at—doubtless a trace of his English upbringing.

He sat with his eyes cast down, and as she watched the patient smile that played about his lips, she felt desperately miserable at having added still further to the burden he had to bear.

"Must I go back now with the memory of having wounded this poor sufferer against my will?" she thought. "I should have more to sorrow for then than I had this morning when I came down to the sea. He must have been a fine young man, with a career before him, and now he has lost all. And he has spent money, given his own work, on this schoolhouse building, to regain the good will of his fellow men. It is hard. I should not have spoken as I did."

Both were silent for the rest of the way home; neither cared to speak.

But when the boat came in to the stone pier under the cliff, and he rose to help her ashore, she grasped his hand.

"Forgive me," she said. "I did not know that it was you."

And she bent down and touched his forehead with her lips.

"What have you done?" he cried, with a look in his eyes as if she had struck him.

"I want you to understand that I do not feel toward you as all the others do," she said.

And, stepping ashore, she walked across the sand without looking backhand in through the pass between the rocks.

But before she had gone many steps, Sven Elversson was at her side, and laid one hand on her arm, that she should stop.

"Thank you ... God bless you ..." he said softly, brokenly. "But remember," he went on, "you must never, never do such a thing again. And you must not tell your husband what you have done. If you told him, then in his jealousy he might kill you."

Sven Elversson was gone, and the young wife walked on alone through the fields, with his last words still in her ears.

"Jealousy!"—could it be true that her husband was jealous? "Oh, heavens, no!" she thought to herself. "It is impossible. He *must* know that I am his with all my soul, with all my thoughts and feelings."

It seemed so cruelly unjust that any one should ever think her husband jealous; the tears rose to her eyes again.

"Heaven knows how it is with that Sven Elversson," she said to herself. "There are many that cannot bear the sight of him, but they all say he is a good man. But perhaps, after all, he is not suffering undeservedly. How could Edward ever be jealous about me? And that was what he was reckoning out to himself while I was talking to him in the boat.

"I wish he were here, so that I could tell him the truth. And the truth is just this—that Edward does not love me any more. It is his misfortune, and mine. But he is not jealous. Oh, a man such as he, so far above all others, who is there he could be jealous of? And that fellow actually thought he could be jealous of him!

"He has ceased to love me," she told herself once more. "He can't help not loving me any more, but he cannot have ceased to believe in me, and in my love for him. It would be too unjust, too blind—it would be almost ridiculous."

On reaching home, the maid came to meet her in the hall, with an anxious face. The service was over already, the Pastor had come back, and was terrified at hearing that his wife was not at home. He had looked for her everywhere; had even been down to the sea to look. He was sitting in his room now—perhaps it would be best to go to him at once.

Fru Rhånge opened the door to the study. What was this?—was he ill? There sat this great strong man, with his face hidden in his arms, rocking to and fro and moaning as if in pain.

She went in, and asked in astonishment what was the matter. But when he looked up, his face was so changed that she hardly knew him—pale and drawn, with dull, bloodshot eyes, and his black beard in ragged wisps about his cheeks. She could hardly have believed such a change was possible in so short a time.

He looked at her with wide eyes, as if not knowing her. Then he passed his hands over his face, trying to control himself, to regain his customary dignity and confident ease. But to no purpose; his emotion was too much for him, and the tears streamed from his eyes.

He stretched out an arm toward her and, without rising, drew her to him. Not a kiss, not a caress; he leaned his head against her breast and sobbed, heartrending to see.

Again and again she begged him to tell her what it was that hurt him, but it was long before he could speak.

And then—nothing more than that he had come home from church and had not found her there; had looked for her about the place, even down to the sea, and, finding her nowhere, he had thought she had given him up and stolen away.

Sigrun could not help giving a little laugh of triumph and satisfaction.

"You must never go away from me again," he said. "You must promise me, now, that you will never leave me. Always let me know where I can find you—you have seen now; I shall go out of my mind if you do not."

And she promised all that he asked. Promised that nothing but death should take her from him.

And then she stood beside him, stroking his hair, till he was himself again. She felt light at heart now that she had had proof of his love. But at the same time there was something strange, something she could not share, in this. It was a love she did not understand—a thing too hot and fierce.

She asked him how he could ever believe she would leave him. And then, impulsively, he told her his thought; she was so far above him. She was from another world, was good in herself, without having to think about it. And he was always fearing that one day she would disappear—he was not good enough to keep her long.

"He does not mean it," she thought to herself. He could not really mean it. It was only his love that exalted her, as love ever will. And in the same way she herself had hitherto exalted him in her heart.

She was no longer miserable and despairing, as she had been in the morning. But there rose up in her a sense of fear toward her husband. And she said no word of having been out sailing with Sven Elversson that day.

Meantime, Sven Elversson and his father were on their way back to Grimön. Old Joel took the tiller, and his son lay in the bows, making himself as comfortable as could be.

Joel had told him of the fire at the school, having heard the news at church. He looked old and bowed and sad; it seemed that now, after this last failure, all ways were closed to his son's advancement.

Sven Elversson stroked his forehead softly as he lay, now with his finger-tips, now with the whole of his slender, delicate hand.

There was a strange sense of freedom and ease in his soul. His thoughts came to him clear and indisputable. He saw his way.

"Father," he said, suddenly, "this loathing is surely the strongest thing of all. No one can overcome it; no one can stand against it. Best to know it from the first. Whoever tries to fight against it must be beaten."

Joel shrugged his shoulders slightly, and grunted out something in answer, but his words were lost in the noise of wind and waves.

Sven lay as before, thinking. And in a little while, when his mind again had given him a clear and indisputable thought, he lifted his voice and cried to his father:

"But loathing is not evil in itself. It is a warning and a safeguard. And if one could use it so, turning it to good use, one might be of great service to mankind."

The old man looked up. His rheumy gray eyes lit up for a moment, and his bowed figure straightened.

Sven sprang to his feet, and, stepping across the thwarts, sat down beside his father.

"Something has happened to me to-day," he said. "Something that has helped me. I am not unhappy now about the fire at the school. I have something else to think of."

Then he went back to his place and lay down again, listening to the heavy rush of the south wind, watching the blending colour of the reefs, and stroking his forehead with his slender, delicate hand.

LESS THAN THE LEAST

JULIUS MARTIN LAMPRECHT, arrested and remanded on a charge of murder, lay on the bench in his cell in the lock-up at Knapefiord, staring into the gray gloom about him.

He was telling himself, as he had done so many times since his arrest, that he was not really guilty, and that there was really no need to confess.

"Now, if I really had been," he said to himself, recollecting his own words at his examination that same morning—"if I really had been guilty of cracking in the skulls of two old people, I should never deny it for a moment. An eye for an eye and a tooth for a tooth—I know about that. And I know that justice must be done. And better to take your punishment in this world than have it to come in the next, where it lasts through all eternity."

The accused was a man about forty-five years of age, and looked almost a giant as he lay there in his cell. His hair was fair and curly as a child's, his complexion had the delicate colouring of youth, with a touch of deeper warmth on the cheeks. A handsome face, on the whole, with well-cut features. Only the eyes, though handsome too in a way, were unprepossessing, with a look in them now staring boldly, now flitting uncertainly from floor to ceiling, from corner to corner.

"Each according to his kind," he thought. "Judges and public prosecutors and that sort must be taken their way. Have to talk a special sort of truth to them, by reason that the real truth cannot reach their hearts, unless it be interpreted unto them."

And all the time he lay here telling himself that he had really committed no murder; he saw himself cold and hungry, dressed in miserable beggar's rags, coming in late one evening to a lonely village hidden away among barren, rocky hills. The door had by accident been left unfastened; he remembered how terrified the old folk had been as they looked up and saw him come in; how hurriedly they had closed the drawer in the table at which they sat. He had spoken kindly, sat down with them by the fire, to warm himself, eaten the food they gave him without hesitation, but aware all the time that they were far from glad of his company, and wished him a thousand miles away.

"And when you happen to be an old convict, sentenced to imprisonment for life, and let out after twenty years of it for exemplary behaviour, it's only natural to be suspected. I can't blame any one for that. I might have thought the same myself." Once more he was quoting from his defence of the morning.

And all the time he saw clearly in his mind's eye how he and the two old people had settled down to rest for the night, they in their bed in one corner, and he on a straw mattress at the other end of the room. The fire was still burning when they went to bed, and he could see the two gray heads side by side. He felt by no means comfortable himself; his bed on the floor was hard and uninviting; he was in ill-humour, and in particular it annoyed him to feel that these two old people grudged him the shelter they could not refuse. The axe that the old man had used to cut a few twigs to put under the pot still lay on the chopping-block; he wondered if it had been left there on purpose, with the blade gleaming in the light of the fire. Easy to find, and ready to hand—was it that?

He began to feel sleepy, but dared not sleep. Once he did so, the old couple would have him at their mercy. The old man, despite his seventy years, looked active enough still. And they were two to one.

He had told them in court that morning, a man who has done his twenty years in prison doesn't want to go back again in a hurry. And really, he ought to be less suspected than others. "But I know it's not that way, as a rule—or, at least, people don't generally act on it."

And as he repeated his well-chosen words he saw himself once more lying on the floor in the little house, straining his ears to listen to the old couplets whispering, the old man urging something, and the woman trying to dissuade him. "Wait till he's asleep," he heard her say. And the vagabond on his hard straw pallet felt more and more uneasy. It was plain that the old couple had money in the house, and were afraid he might steal it. There's a power of danger more than folk would think in the life of a poor vagabond.

And he was cautious, and pretended to go to sleep, and snored loudly, waiting to see what they would do. The old man said his prayers, and that was all; but that in itself was a masterly piece of deceit to one who knew what they had in mind—one who could see how the blade of the axe shone in the light of the dying fire, all ready to hand—one who understood well enough that they were only trying to lull his suspicion to rest.

"But," thought the accused, "you can't get a judge to believe a thing like that. Won't hear a word of self-defence, especially when it's a poor wanderer coming all unarmed and helpless into a strange house. But, for my part, I can't call it murder at all. If I hadn't got up and smashed in their skulls, they'd have smashed in mine. I don't believe they were asleep at all, though they lay quite still and never moved. It was all a sham. And if I'd been fool enough to go off to sleep myself in earnest, what would have happened then? They'd have been up and out of bed in a moment, with the axe. And after, what could be easier than to bury a body and hide it up, in a wild place like that? No, it's almost wicked to tempt people, having it all so easy."

And each time the accused went over in his mind the events of that night he felt more and more convinced that he had only killed the two old people in self-defence.

At first, he had not expected to be arrested at all. In the first place, the village where the two old people lay asleep, each with a cloven skull, was far off the high road, and he had every hope that nothing would be discovered until he was far away in safety. Then, too, he had so thoroughly persuaded himself of his innocence that he felt Providence must protect him. For the justice of Providence is other than that of courts of law on earth. It was a justice that understood how a poor vagabond might be forced to act in self-defence. With that sort of justice it was possible, so to speak, to talk as man to man.

The only thing this supreme justice could reasonably reproach him with was—he admitted it freely—a little white lie or so that he had allowed himself to tell at the examination, with regard to where he had been on the night of the crime and the days following. But for all his conscientiousness and his love of right and justice, he realized that in his case it was pardonable. For when a man had been arrested in despite of common fairness and humanity, merely because he happened to have been in prison before—and possibly also to some extent because a savings-bank book, the property of the deceased, and been found on his person—why, he was simply forced to deviate a little from the strict and literal truth. He had been obliged to confess that he had stolen the bank book from the pocket of a fellow passenger in the train. He had not endeavoured to assert that it had been honestly come by, but had freely confessed he had stolen it. As to where the other traveller had obtained it—who could say? It was too much to ask that he, the accused, show know the goings and comings of every stranger.

Again and again he went through the same arguments, each time feeling himself more and more innocent of any crime.

He had reached so far, indeed, as to be filled with an intense conviction of having barely, by a miracle of grace, escaped being murdered in his sleep himself—when the door of his cell opened, and the notary, who had conducted the proceedings of that morning, stepped in, followed by two other men. One was the warder, who had been deputed to look after him, and the other a young man, dressed like a workman of the better class.

The prisoner rose at once to his feet, with an air of respectful attention. He was resolved, as he had told the prison chaplain, on all occasions to observe a proper demeanour, and show that he himself was not only a lover of justice, but well disposed toward its servants.

"I have to inform you, Lamprecht," said the young notary, "that your case will be decided to-morrow. And once more I would ask you, while there is yet time, to ease your conscience and obtain a lighter sentence by sincere repentance and confession."

The accused answered only with a determined shake of the head, but for the rest maintained an attitude of tolerant understanding.

"I can understand, of course, that the notary finds it difficult," he said. "I have myself learned to love justice, which is the foundation of all society—the one thing in which all must trust. And I can understand that it seems hard to judge. You do not wish to condemn an innocent man, or, on the other hand, to let the guilty escape."

While he was speaking he noticed that the judge made a gesture with his hand once or twice as if to interrupt, but he took no heed. A man who has spent twenty years in prison has gained a certain amount of experience in the time, and may have various things to say which might be useful to a notary acting, perhaps for the first time, as judge.

He was allowed to finish what he had to say. Then the judge went on, entirely unmoved.

"You find it very difficult to give clear and distinct answers to questions put. And I have therefore written down these three points which you have to answer." He took up a paper, and held it toward the accused, reading out the contents at the same time:

"'Do you, Julius Martin Lamprecht, confess to having murdered Jonas Mikaelson with an axe on the night following the twelfth of February 1909?

"'Do you, Julius Martin Lamprecht, confess to having murdered Brita Gustava, wife of the aforesaid Jonas Mikaelson, with an axe on the night following the twelfth of February 1909?

"'Do you, Julius Martin Lamprecht, confess to having been aware that the two persons aforesaid possessed a bank book showing a deposit of two hundred *kronor*, and to having committed the murder in order to gain possession of the same?'"

The notary laid the paper on the table.

"You can think it over," he said. "You know that there is no prospect of your being acquitted, but a confession given of your own free will may lead to a mitigation of the sentence. Here is the paper; I will have pen and ink brought in."

The accused was by no means pleased at the manner in which his mode of expressing himself had been criticized; he was indeed altogether out of humour now. He stared blankly before him.

"You heard what I said?" the notary went on. "You understand that there are three questions here for you to answer, with your signature?"

The accused drew a deep breath. He was annoyed, and made no attempt to hide it. He spat on the paper and going back to his bench, lay down and closed his eyes.

"I will have a new copy of the paper brought in at once," said the judge as calmly as before.

"You have an hour. I shall wait in the building that time for your answer. You are too fond of delay and prevarication; I intend to show you that the time for such evasions is now past."

The accused answered only with an oath.

A moment after, he heard the door open, and imagined that the visitors had left. He did not trouble himself to open his eyes and look.

"That slip of a boy will never dare to condemn me," he thought. "Not as long as I stick to a firm denial. As for his paper, I've no need to answer that. Why should I?"

And, lying stretched on his bench, he saw in his mind's eye the same scenes as he had seen before; repeated his former arguments, growing ever more and more convinced of his entire innocence. He was certain now that the two old villagers had been in the habit of laying traps for lonely wanderers; they must have had more than one such life on their conscience.

At the same time, he found something pleasant in the thought that the judge had come in person to ask him to confess. It was proof that they regarded him as an important and dangerous man, whom they were loth to release.

"There you are!" he said to himself proudly. "That's how it is. People all round are afraid the murderer may escape after all. All that crowd there was in the court this morning. And the papers taking it up so eagerly. And the judge himself uncertain what to do; yes, it's all easy enough to understand. They'd like to condemn, but they haven't proof enough. And so they're trying to wring out a confession to help them. They know they can't condemn a man without proof as long as he denies it and sticks to it."

He felt so sure of his safety now that he began to whistle.

Perhaps, after all, it might turn out that this sore trial had not been in vain. "After this," he thought to himself, "there'll be no need to be content with cold potatoes and scrapings of porridge when you come to a lonely hut. After this, you'll only have to say your name, Julius Martin Lamprecht, and people 'll know what they've got to do. They'll get busy then, soon enough, with pots and pans on the fire, and serve up the best they've got. No more lying on a bit of mattress on the floor; no, it 'll be the visitor, the stranger within their gates, that sleeps in the best bed, and the others can sleep on the floor or out in the shed, if they like."

But here the accused was again interrupted in his train of thought. A quiet, gentle voice close by him:

"Five minutes have gone already."

He opened his eyes. The man dressed like a workman, who had followed the others into the cell, stood by his side, watch in hand, pointing to the dial as he spoke.

"What are you doing here? Who are you?" cried the accused, unpleasantly surprised to find that he was not alone. He wondered uneasily if he had been thinking aloud.

"I—I am nobody to speak of," said the other. "My name is Sven Elversson, son of Joel Elversson from Grimön. But it just occurred to me that you might perhaps fall off to sleep, or forget about the time, until it was too late. And so I asked them to let me stay in here and talk to you."

Lamprecht could find nothing to disapprove of in the stranger. There was something extremely humble about his manner, his smile, the tone of his voice. Even the way his hair was done seemed to have something of humility about it. He was clean-shaven, too, which added to the impression. All that could indicate selfishness, pride, superiority, was effaced. "Must be one of those well-meaning folk that go about doing good," thought the prisoner to himself. "Well, he won't get much out of me, anyhow."

"D'you think for a moment I'm ever going to write a word on that paper there?" he asked, scornfully.

"Do not say 'no' before you've had time to think," said Sven Elversson, with a glance of gentle humility and goodness. "You have had dealings with the law before, and you know well enough that you cannot be condemned in this court as long as you persist in a denial; they will have to acquit you for lack of proof. But before you decide, let me tell you that there are certain persons here who have ordered the sum of five thousand kronor to be placed at your disposal if you decide to confess. There is reason to believe that you would be glad of the money, although you will not, of course, be able to spend it yourself."

The accused felt a sudden shiver through his body from head to foot. At the same time, he could not help making a grimace. But he pulled himself together.

"What the devil is that you say?" he cried.

"Yes, it is true," said Sven Elversson. "We are ready to give you that money, if you confess. You understand that it is a matter of importance to us others that you should confess? Everyone in the district, perhaps in the whole country, is horrified. And we have resolved that you shall not go about the country asking for shelter of lonely folk if we can help it. That must not be. It is too great a temptation for a man like you. We want you imprisoned for life. We wish you no harm beyond that. We have no wish to take your life, or to hurt you at all, but we must have you in confinement. I and several others have watched you in court, and heard what you said. You are not exactly an intentional criminal, but you have fancies, and are easily frightened; you imagine that everyone is anxious to harm you. And if you think over it carefully, you will see that it is best for yourself that you should be shut up. You will be at peace then, and need have no fear of any one. I think, then, it would be better for you and for everyone else if you were to accept the five thousand kronor and confess."

"Not for a hundred thousand!" exclaimed the accused.

Sven Elversson had drawn gradually closer to the man while speaking, and sat down now on the bench beside him.

"Do not say that," he urged kindly, laying one hand on the other's sleeve. "Five thousand kronor is a good sum, and fully enough for the purpose for which you would use it. You cannot say otherwise. More would not be good for the one who is to have the money, and less would hardly do. Five thousand is as good as could be."

"I can't make you out," said the accused. "What do you think I should use it for? Who is the one I should give it to?"

"I am glad you asked me that," said Sven Elversson. "It was of that I wished to speak to you. There has been a great deal about you in the papers of late, and, among other things, how you are always asking after your daughter wherever you go. You were married, it seemed, before you committed that first murder two and twenty years ago, and on your release you tried at once to find out where your wife was. But she was dead. But you had a daughter—she would be a little over twenty now, and, as far as any one knows, she is alive, but no one could tell you where she had gone. And so you have been wandering about the country looking for her everywhere. As soon as you entered a house, the first thing you did was always to ask if any there knew anything of Julia Lamprecht. And"—here Sven lowered his voice and went on a little sadly—"it seemed to me that there was something I liked about that. There must be something good in a man who went about seeking for his daughter."

"But in the name of Heaven," cried the accused, "what have you to do with it all? Why are you here, talking to me like this? Can't you tell me what it is you want with me?"

"Thanks once more," said Sven Elversson in his gentlest voice, as if fearing to arouse the other's displeasure. "Those are just questions that I shall be only too glad to answer. I am from Grimön, as I said—a little island far out at sea, so far, at any rate, that I myself need have no fear of you, for you would hardly come there. But I have a mother who has warnings in her dreams at times. And on the morning of the thirteenth of February she asked me to go over to the mainland and see how things were with an old couple—relatives of ours—who lived in a little cottage among the stonehills, far from the high road, and with no neighbours near. She had dreamed something that made it seem best for someone to go and see how they were. And I did as she asked me. And so it came about that I was the first to discover what you had done that night. And I will not deny that it was a cruel sight, and ever since I have wished something could be done to prevent you from ever being free to go about again. And that is why I have been about collecting this money. I wish you no harm, do not think that. I have told you so already. I only want to see you imprisoned now for life."

As he spoke, he moved a little closer, and stroked the other's sleeve gently. He was evidently anxious that Lamprecht should not think he bore him any personal ill will. Had the man been a lion escaped from its cage, its keeper might have coaxed it back behind the bars in the same way.

It would be untrue to say that the accused did not regard him with uneasiness. Everyone filled him with uneasiness: judge and gaoler, magistrate and witnesses. But he could not help feeling that this Sven Elversson was little to be feared—he seemed, indeed, something weak in his mind. "One of those fellows that go about doing good," he told himself again. "Philanthropists, they call them."

"I seem to understand a little now," he said aloud. "As soon as you found out that I went about looking for my daughter you thought you could use her as a bait to catch a poor fellow again for good."

And he laughed in Sven's soft face. The lion was determined to keep its freedom, and cared nothing for the bait offered.

"Thank you," said Sven Elversson, with his humblest smile. "What you say brings me just to the very thing I wanted to tell you. Look you, last summer I was doing some building work in the district. Not for myself, you understand, but to order. And I had to get some stone from a quarry just above the fishing village of Knapefiord, where we are now, and in that way I came into contact with a good many of the people there. And among them was a young woman named Julia Lamprecht. It was an unusual name, and as soon as I saw your name in the papers I remembered her."

The accused rose to his feet. Again he felt that shiver through his body. His face twitched, his eyelids quivered; it was evident that some emotion took possession of him at the mention of his daughter, though, truth to tell, he had been seeking her hitherto less from any warmth of real feeling than in the hope that she might perhaps be well off and able to give him a home.

He thrust Sven Elversson aside carelessly, and stood up in the middle of the cell.

"Is she here?" he asked. "I want to see her."

His tone was that of a man who expects immediate obedience to his orders. But Sven Elversson did not lose countenance.

"You shall see her," he said, kindly and gently as before, but not without firmness. "You shall sit and talk with her as you are doing now with me. But there is one thing to be done first. You must write the answers on that paper. You may think, perhaps, that we are cruel in trying to separate father and daughter in this way, but we must have that paper signed first."

The accused flushed angrily. He was not accustomed to have any reasonable request refused. Ever since he had been arrested, he had been treated with the greatest leniency, to make him thrive, as it were, in captivity, and render him more willing to give the confession that would keep him there. He felt now as if he could spring at this stranger and thrash him soundly, but he controlled himself. He threw himself face downward on the bench, keeping his face hidden. He did not know himself what made him do so, but he felt it was best to conceal his feelings.

"I am glad, I am grateful to you for thinking it over," said Sven. "I must tell you that Julia Lamprecht is not very happy as she is. Her mother died early, as you know. And since then she has, as one might say, grown up in the streets. She came here in company with a workman from the quarries. They were not married, but quarrymen hereabouts do not always trouble about marrying, so no one paid much heed to that. And Julia is a good girl; there are many worse than she. But a few days back, when the man heard she was your daughter, he left her. Couldn't bear the sight of her, he said. And now she is all alone. She is handsome, like her father, with fair hair, and no doubt there will be others ready to be friends with her in a way, but it will only be the same again. Now, if she had a little money, say five thousand kroner, then she could buy a little house and be properly married. Five thousand would be just about right. More would not be well for her, and less would be hardly enough. Well, now you see how we have thought it out. As soon as you have answered the questions there, you can see her, and give her the five thousand. You would like that, I think. Then she would feel she had a father. She would feel that, whatever you might have done, you had still some affection for her."

The accused was silent for a long time. He moved to and fro restlessly on the bench, moaning from time to time. There was, after all, something in the man that cried for his child. Fair, handsome, like her father, she was. And perhaps even then sitting outside and waiting....

Suddenly he sat up, brushed his hair from his forehead, and looked Sven Elversson straight in the face.

"Can you tell me," he said, "why I should write on that paper at all? I shall be acquitted to-morrow."

"Quite likely," answered Sven, "you may be acquitted of the murder. But then there is that other matter of the bank book. In any case, you will not be released yet awhile. It may be years before you are a free man again. You cannot say how long it may be. And, in the meantime, what is to happen to the girl? She may be ruined before you see her. It is not an easy thing for a girl to be the daughter of such a man as you. And I am afraid she will go from bad to worse. Five thousand now, that would help her. Let her have the money now, and you will have something to think of, something to be glad of, all your life. Then you will have done something to wipe out what you have done. You would be respected for that."

The accused rose to his feet once more.

"Stop it!" he cried, stamping his foot. "You are driving me out of my mind with your talk."

Sven was silent at once.

The accused stood thinking, searching out his soul; looking everywhere for that love for his daughter that he thought must be there. They were trying to lead him as they pleased through his love for his daughter. They asked of him to sacrifice all that was left of life for her sake. He, a man with nothing in the world but his freedom, he was to give up that for his daughter's sake! For love of her! But was there any such love in him at all? Now that he sought for it, he could find nothing. Or yes, perhaps, a little. But nothing to speak of. Not enough to make a sacrifice. It is not so easy to make sacrifices. This fellow here who talked so glibly about it all, and was trying all the time to get him shut up and put out of harm's way—would he make any sacrifice for the sake of what he sought?

"I will do as you ask," he said at last; "I will answer those three questions. But on one condition. It's all very well that my girl gets the money. But the money's not everything after all. No, the best thing she could have would be a good husband. *If you will promise me to marry her yourself, then I will sign.*"

Sven Elversson started back in consternation.

"I had not expected that," he said in a low voice.

"I am asking if you will marry my daughter," said the accused, with a sneer. "Now, what do you say to that? You ask me to give up everything for her sake, but you are not so ready to give up anything yourself."

"But—she is your daughter. It was you that brought her into the world," said Sven Elversson. "I have hardly spoken to her in my life."

"Just as you like. Only then, of course, I need not trouble about the questions. It's really a pity, though. I've quite taken a fancy to you. I'd like to have you for a son-in-law." And he laughed boisterously.

Sven Elversson passed his hand over his eyes, and drew a deep breath. "I understand now," he said to himself. "The man who would have power over others must be prepared to crucify himself. Nothing less will serve."

He looked long and searchingly at the man before him.

"He is trying to get out of it," he thought. "And wants to lay the blame on me. He is sure I should refuse. But I will not refuse. I have him cornered now, and I will not let him go."

"Let it be as you say," he said, shortly. "If your daughter will have me, I will marry her. Now write!"

The accused man hesitated.

"Very kind of you, I'm sure," he said. "But how am I to know you will keep your word?"

"Of course," said Sven. "I was waiting for you to ask that. Now, if you think a moment, you will understand that in a place like this walls have ears. There are witnesses already to the fact that I have promised to marry Julia Lamprecht, provided that she consents. I cannot escape now. As long as I wish to be looked on as an honourable man, I cannot escape. Now, sit down at the table and write!"

Lamprecht sat down at the table. He took up the pen, dipped it in the ink, and groaned.

Sitting there, pen in hand, he sought once more for that love for his daughter. It might, perhaps, have been there in his soul at the time when he hoped to find a home with her, but now—now that he was asked to give up his freedom for her sake, it was nowhere to be found.

He wrote with the pen upright, and with the pen aslant; dipped again and again, splashed the ink about, and at last it was done.

"All I ever promised you was to *answer* the questions," he said, and handed Sven Elversson the paper.

And Sven Elversson read, and saw that the judge's three questions were answered with three crooked, straggling words: "*No*" and "*No*" and "*No.*" Beneath was the signature, Julius Martin Lamprecht, and finally a single sentence, rambling and ill-spelt: "I would confess if I was guilty, but I am not."

"You will not get the five thousand kronor for that," said Sven Elversson, quietly.

"I didn't suppose so," returned the other. "But I've got you to marry my girl. I never promised you but I would answer the questions if you agreed to marry my daughter. And I've done it. I'll be acquitted, and I've got a good husband for her."

He stood there throwing out his chest, proud of his victory.

Sven Elversson flushed angrily. His humility had disappeared, and his manner toward the accused was less kind than before.

"I might have thought it," he said. "I ought to have known what a scoundrel you were. I have seen how you treated those two poor creatures after you had killed them. What made you put out their eyes?" he asked passionately.

"Put out their eyes!" cried the accused. "That's not true. Someone else must have done that. When I left them — —"

He broke off, bit his lips, and staggered, pale as death, to the wall of the cell.

"Thanks," said Sven Elversson drily. "I knew how I could get you, if need should be. But I waited, as long as there was a chance, to make it easier for you."

Next moment the murderer lay on his knees before him.

"I didn't say it; I didn't say anything," he cried. "I didn't say it—it doesn't count—you tricked me!"

The man was suddenly transformed to a miserable, grovelling heap of penitence and despair. All his armour of conceit and self-deception, all his subterfuges and excuses, had been torn from him now.

"There are witnesses here, as I told you before," said Sven Elversson. "I warned you."

"I'll write it again—give me a new paper and I'll confess. I'll tell you all, I'll do all you ask, for the sake of the girl."

Sven Elversson raised his voice a little.

"I will tear up this paper," he said. "Another shall be brought directly. And if the new one is properly answered and signed, then I fancy the walls will have heard nothing of the first. We will start again from the moment you sat down to write. The hour is not yet gone. You, Julius Martin Lamprecht, have still time to make a free confession."

A little later, the murderer sat on a chair in his cell, facing the judge. His appearance was changed; he wore the look of a man washed and cleansed, though no such process had taken place outwardly. But he had confessed. Not only had he answered the two first questions in the affirmative, and the last in the negative, but he had delivered a full and free confession of the whole affair. He was exhausted now, and a chair had to be brought for him or he would have fallen to the floor. But for all that he looked happy and content. At that moment he bore no ill will to any living soul. He was cleansed and freed from sin. He had not felt such comfort since his first communion.

In addition to the judge, there were present in the cell a warder, a constable, the clerk, and Julia Lamprecht, and Sven Elversson. The prisoner loved them all, and most of all his daughter, to whom he had just given the sum of five thousand kronor. He found her beautiful to look at. Handsome, fair, with curly hair, and a queer shyness of manner. He had not yet spoken with her alone, but the judge had promised she should be allowed to sit in his cell as long as he pleased.

Now and again the murderer turned his eyes toward the man who had forced him to confess, and he could not help feeling a certain sympathy with him.

The very look of the man, as he stood there leaning against the cell wall, with his eyes cast down and his brow gloomily furrowed, was enough to inspire sympathy. The murderer felt he understood him better than any other. He, Lamprecht, a murderer, could confess his crime and atone for it, but this man would never be able to wipe away the stain that clung to his name.

The murderer had seen how the judge and all the other servants of the law had shaken hands with Sven Elversson and thanked him. The judge, especially, had been profoundly grateful. It was a great relief to him now to be able to give his decision without hesitation.

But Sven Elversson looked as humble and sad as ever—only more humble, if anything, than before. He looked like a man utterly weary of himself.

When Julia Lamprecht entered the cell to receive the five thousand kronor, Sven Elversson had stepped forward and declared that he had promised the prisoner to make his daughter an offer of marriage. But the girl had refused at once. She would not marry that man—never. And she had told him plainly what manner of man he was.

Sven Elversson had been deeply hurt at her refusal. It seemed to torture him. He drew back without a word, and stood leaning unsteadily against the cell wall. And the prisoner himself felt that he was revenged.

His daughter, whom he had never seen until that day, had taken vengeance on the man who had conquered her father. He felt she was of his blood, and he loved her.

Not that he repented of his confession. He felt clean and easy in mind, happy and respected, almost like a decent man. And he had seen his daughter, whom he would love now all his life, and who would always love him, since he had given up his freedom for her sake.

As for the true confession, the murderer passed it over, erased it from his memory. He was a man who always needed to look at himself in a good light. He was already busy in his mind with a beautiful and touching story of how it was for this daughter's sake alone he had confessed, and prayed to God and man for forgiveness. As long as he lived, he would be able to weave that story over and over again, and he would believe it, and it would serve to maintain his self-respect during the long, hard years that awaited him.